Spook

Spook

Steve Vance

1 Union Square
New York, NY 10003

Library of Congress Cataloging-in-Publication Data
Vance, Steve, 1952–
Spook / Steve Vance
p.   cm.
ISBN 0–939149–38–9
I. Title
PS3572.A4245S6   1990   90–40469
813'.54—dc20   CIP AC

Manufactured in the United States

To Brenda, who did so much of the work;
to Jackie, who put up with crazy penpals; and
to Marlys, who is partially responsible
for the results.

Spook

THEIR SPINES rattled as the night breeze swayed the stalks of winter corn on which she had hung them all around the earthen circle. The sharp moonlight made the bones glow. As the wind picked up, they gently danced and clacked. In the tin wash tub, suspended over the larger of the shallow pits, the water came to a boil. It was time.

The girl went to the cage and reached in for the white rabbit huddled at the back, terrified. The eyes gleamed, even in the dark. She took it by the scruff and eased it out, then sat on the ground, the creature in her lap. She petted it. Not too long, she thought.

The rabbit's ears lay flat against its luxuriant fur. It wasn't often that she trapped a white one. Around her wrist was the loop of wire. Gently she slipped it over the soft neck and slowly drew it closed, like a collar. The rabbit's heart beat against her hand, its body warming her palm even as it shook with its small terrors. With a practiced motion, she brought the wooden handles up and around to the back all the while petting. Then yanked. The circle snapped closed.

The rabbit screeched and thrashed, desperately flailing. She held the knobs of the garrote taut with one hand, grasping the rabbit's chest fur with the other. Its lungs bellowed uselessly. Drops of warm blood fell from its mouth onto her wrist. It took nearly a minute. The axe would have been quicker but would have ruined the bones.

There was scurrying in the woods. The death cry had brought the dogs. They weren't hungry, only suspicious, and anxious for sport now as they picked up the smell. She slid the carcass whole into the pot at the bottom of the shallow pit and squatted down on the rim. Embers rose up like insects and shot skyward. The liquid boiled. It would take many hours for the flesh to separate from the skeleton.

She looked to the moon to check the hour, then stared wistfully at the dark slope that led to the paved road. She wanted to see the humans who had camped by the drainage tunnel. Perhaps they had something she needed. Maybe she would be lucky again and find a young couple whom she might watch from the darkness. She was so drawn to the sinewy white flesh, the way it bunched beneath the skin, then smoothed, the light cries they emitted when bitten.

She splayed her fingers, ordering the dogs to stay, and padded down the path. Even in the pitch blackness beneath the trees she had no trouble making her way. Her bare feet knew every rock and stump.

At the bottom of the slope, she came to the road. The moonlight shone upon the skunk's stripe down its middle.

Keeping to the shoulder, she trod quietly the quarter mile to the drainage pipe, slowing as she neared. The light of a fire flickered from inside the pipe but she could sense no one about. Pausing, she listened. Nothing, not even breathing. The smoke made it hard to smell anything. Nonetheless, she was confident no one occupied the makeshift campsite.

The summer past she had been lucky in just such a situation, and had gotten the small, light axe she so loved. Perhaps they had something as fine. She checked again to make sure no one was nearby and moved toward the mouth of the pipe. At the entrance, she paused and listened again, then slipped inside, one eye shut to preserve its usefulness in the dark.

She knew instantly from the smell of their bedding that there would be nothing. They had nothing.

"Hey, doll," a voice said. She turned, crouched like a trapped animal. "What are you doing in here?"

The man stood in the opening, slightly bent, both arms raised, hands pressed against the top of the pipe.

"What's that sack on your head for?" He looked back over his shoulder to somebody else. "Treg," he called, "Treg," as he started to enter the tunnel. "Willya look't this. We got a night visitor."

She moved to the side, away from the fire, her shadow large on the curve of the wall.

"Other side, Treg. Other side." He smiled. "She ain't got no underwear."

He came toward her, hands out, palms up, making a soothing groan. She stood to her full height as he approached. The other man's footfalls were scratchy on the tarmac; he was atop the roadbed that straddled the pipe.

"You're a tall one," the man said, voice still silken. "Ain't you cold, darlin'—barefoot and all? Ey, are you winkin' at me, you cutie?"

He looked surprised as her fingers clamped his windpipe, driving the Adam's apple back into his voice box. His hands flew to his throat. He choked, eyes rheumy, face crimson. Released, he fell onto the incline of the wall, gurgling, legs thrashing, unable to escape the pain in his body.

She smothered the fire with their blankets and opened her other eye.

The second man shouted into the tunnel from the far end, his voice concerned. Hearing the gagging, he entered the pipe, slightly bent. He snapped on a small flashlight the size of a pen. His friend crawled toward him on his bottom, like a baby, hands around his throat. The second man drew a knife and walked slowly forward. The smoke stung. He walked cautiously down the middle of the pipe, all the way to the opening. The tunnel was empty.

WAVES SLIPPED onto the beach a little faster, a little more insistently. Their sound carried across the sand to fill the beach house. Barbara Abbott rolled over in bed, closer to him, and smiled with that gauzy, gorgeous look that was a mix of clinging sleep and the very real love she held for this man.

"Hi," she purred.

Eric grinned, slowly, warmly, eyes still closed. It was only a little past six. Rolling westward, the morning light rose easily out of the south Atlantic coloring the room and their skin.

She was 19, twenty years younger than Eric Halliday. He was poor; she was rich, the daughter of a Miami Beach hotel magnate. She was blonde, blue-eyed, knockout beautiful, and the target of countless South Florida hustlers. But she had early on acquired a canny immunity to the smooth talk of the pretty boys who prowled the exclusive beachfront places. Only Eric—slender, unemployed, soulful—had captured her heart from the moment they'd met in an art gallery three months before.

With his long, reddish-brown hair and beard, he looked like the last flower child, but when he spoke of things like inner peace and harmonic convergence, you had to believe every word, because there was no room for dishonesty in this man. Barbara became more sure of the goodness in him each time they made love. Their gentle ease was extraordinary, she thought. It was right; she knew instinctively that it was so right.

She sighed, her eyes closed. So what if her dad didn't approve of Eric. What parent would. She didn't think much of her father's second and third wives either, so he was hardly in a position to judge.

Eric kissed her forehead. "Have a good night?"

"Wonderful," she said. "Wonderful dreams."

He said, contentedly, "It's going to be a terrific day today."

Barbara yawned happily. Just about every day she'd spent with Eric had been terrific, but this was going to be the best yet. Today she would tell him. Now, in fact.

"Baby," she said. "Give me your hand."

Eric Halliday looked a little bemused in the thin morning light. Lying on his side, he extended his hand. When she took it and kissed it, he eased closer. She touched his chest to stop him.

"Honey. I want to tell you something."

Eric raised his eyebrows. "What?"

She placed his hand on her smooth midriff.

"I think," he said, "we're verging on something nice here."

"Do you feel it?" she said.

"You know I do."

She laughed. "I mean, do you feel what we've done. What our love has made for us?"

He paused, leaned back a little bit, his smile intact but a tiny change in his eyes. "You mean . . . a baby?"

Barbara closed her eyes and nodded slowly. This then was the start of her second life and by far the more important one.

"What happened?" Eric murmured. "You said the Pill never caused you problems."

"It doesn't, but I knew there was only one surefire way to win over Daddy, and this is it. He really wants grandkids in the worst way. And now he'll have them, and I'll have you. The doctor confirmed it yesterday." A sudden fear cut into the moment; her eyes opened wide. "You do love me, don't you, Eric?"

But his expression was totally affectionate.

"You'll never need to ask me that, Barbie, because I'll love you even after I'm dead. Never doubt that."

She breathed deeply, relieved and overjoyed. "And you want our baby?"

"As much as I want you," he said, and kissed the tip of her nose.

Warm tears filled her. "Oh, Jesus. I love you so much, you know."

His kiss silenced her, and after they sweetly made love again, she drifted back to sleep on the sounds of the surf. A little after seven he slipped so quietly out of bed that Barbara didn't stir from her dreams of him.

ERIC SAT in the station waiting nervously for the arrival of the next bus. He had lifted enough cash from her purse to purchase a plane ticket back home to California, but he was afraid that her old man would expect him to bolt in that direction, and would have well-dressed guys with broken noses staking out all the airports. With all that damn Abbott money and clout, the bastard could afford to do a thorough job of it, too.

So he had headed instead for the bus station. Who would ever expect a fleeing expectant father to ride a bus out of town?

Eric Halliday picked up a news magazine from a table and stared at it. Nothing registered. He couldn't concentrate, and threw it back. Damn! Why had she pulled a stupid stunt like that? They could have had all summer together, a great time, and he would have made certain that it was every bit as good for her. But no, she had to make a goddamned unilateral decision.

Without his volition, the memory of her father's last edict snapped into his mind: Listen to me, you skinny, over-aged shithead. If you get my little girl knocked up, I'm going to make sure that you never have the means of doing it to any other little girls. Get my meaning?

Eric got it. "Damn," he whispered aloud.

Maybe he could have told Barbara to have the pregnancy taken care of. No, that wouldn't have worked. As one of Miami's most idle and richest offspring, she didn't have to worry about the financial considerations of raising a child, and she tended to take a negative view of abortion.

"Love me, love my baby," he muttered, looking at his watch.

He might have stayed in Miami and fought for a part of that beautiful Abbott family fortune. He wasn't getting any younger –forty come October. He wouldn't see thirty-nine and a half anytime soon again. Spending his declining years in the lap of luxury wasn't so terrible a fate, he supposed. If he and Barbara had slipped away and had a quiet ceremony, probably even Papa Abbott would have accepted him. But . . . the memento he'd left Barbara was hardly the only such keepsake in his past. There were probably five or six little likenesses bouncing around somewhere out there, and if any of their mothers happened to discover that old sweet-talking Eric had bagged himself a wealthy and socially prominent family . . . well, the fun would be over. They would descend on him.

In spite of the depressing dilemma, Eric Halliday couldn't suppress a flash of a grin. There was another reason, too, that he wasn't ready to nestle into the smothering arms of matrimony. He had been more places and seen more things than twenty average guys, but he didn't feel that he was even halfway through his life's vagabond itinerary, and he wasn't about to waste any of himself on domestic bliss. At least not while his legs were strong.

Through the open doors, he heard a Greyhound bus pull up out front, its brakes hissing like the lungs of a surfacing whale. Eric clutched the backpack that contained all of the things he owned or cared to own. He looked at the bus as it gleamed in the early morning sun. He didn't know where the thing was heading, but instinct told him that it was going his way.

THE BUS carried him north from Miami without problems. But near Jacksonville, Daddy Abbott's big-money reach displayed itself.

The bus pulled into a truckstop for dinner, just on the outskirts of the city. Darkness had reduced the sun to a thin red crescent on the western horizon. Although the driver assured his overnight passengers that their belongings were safe on the bus, Eric Halliday had the presence of mind to carry his backpack with him. Never one to linger over a meal, Eric had finished his burger and fries, and taken care of business in the restroom, when the two state patrol cars pulled into the parking lot with their lights flashing but sirens quiet.

His hands still wet from the busted wall-dryer, he stopped wiping them on his jeans when he saw the state heat through the wide front windows. Could they be looking for him? Not likely.

One of the black-booted troopers stepped into the bus and scanned the interior. Son of a bitch. Eric cursed, swinging his pack over one shoulder. They might be looking for dope or underage runaways, or escaped mass murderers, or any of a dozen other things. But he wasn't going to gamble his freedom on coincidence. As the driver crossed the diner to meet the officers at the door, Eric Halliday slipped by a startled waitress into the kitchen and sprinted for the back door.

He was lucky, and very fast. There was a thick outcropping of trees no more than fifty yards from the back and he reached the treeline before the thick-headed state boys ever realized that they should be chasing him. He heard the screen door bang several times, and some loud voices, but by then he was deep into the grove. Gone.

He kept on moving all night. By daybreak, he had walked and hitched his way across the line into Georgia. For a few days, he decided, he would stick to hitching, both to ease the pressure on his cash, and to allow the bus lines to forget his looks, just in case Abbott's influence extended beyond Florida. Hitchhiking onto I-75 went alright, but from there on his luck ran out.

The long-haired, soulful look, that worked so well with the babes, failed to work its spell on the passing truckers. To them he was a pony-tailed scuzz. And most of the civilian traffic that slowed down to check him out, had occupants that he didn't care to chance riding with. So it took three full days to get from Jacksonville to Duncan County, Georgia, a township forty miles south of the Tennessee line.

Welcome to Duncan County, he thought, birthplace of the word "bucolic." The worst part was that he was off the interstate highway. The last sucker to pick him up had used one hand to keep the car somewhere near the right lane, while, with the other hand, he'd drained a hip flask. The drunk swung off the interstate, ignoring his passenger's request to be dropped on the highway. He assured Eric they'd resume their journey north as soon as his liquor was replenished.

Eric Halliday certainly didn't want to be eyeballed by the Peach State's finest at some beer joint with this guy. When the fool stopped in the middle of a deserted two-lane road to puke, Eric slipped out. The drunk didn't even seem to notice as he cranked up again and cruised off, shimmying from side to side, roughly following the yellow line.

Eric was safely on foot again, but he didn't have a ghost of an idea where he was. He wasn't even sure, after their meandering drive, which direction to take back to I-75. With a sigh, he began to walk.

No houses, no streetlamps, no roadsigns, not even smashed beer bottles and road trash. Just the blacktop, the cold air, and a narrow strip of moonless, star-dusted sky, running between the partitions of pine trees on either side of the road. "Man," he said aloud, his shoes crunching loose gravel.

He walked for nearly half an hour before he heard the first car approaching from behind. Quickly he stepped across the ditch at the side of the road to check out the approaching vehicle before its driver caught sight of him.

It didn't look like a cop car, at least not a marked one, and it seemed to be soberly driven, albeit fast. Real fast. Still, in the middle of Nowhere, USA, how many rides would he have to choose from. With a shrug, he stepped back across onto the road apron and stuck out his thumb, smiling.

The car shot past, its headlights blazing on high-beam. Not a touch on the brakes. "Damn."

In the brief instant before being blinded, he thought the lone occupant was small and long-haired, probably female. Not much chance a woman would stop for him out here at night, but it still jerked his chain. "I hope your oil pan drops off!" he shouted after the diminishing taillights. It didn't help. He allowed himself a few moments to stand and stew, then took up the slow trek in the same direction the car had taken and hoped it was the way to the interstate.

IT WAS real cold tonight, like maybe Spring had forgotten that it was supposed to last through May. And it was going to rain. She could smell that.

Maybe I'll stay inside, in the warm, she thought. Mama all the time says I should stay inside.

The girl lay on her back, gazing at the stars, new ones every night, even when it seemed the sky itself couldn't hold them all. She stretched her hand up into the cold darkness to pluck one down. The star backed away, she thought. Everything moved away from her, always. Her fingers closed into a hard ball. Clouds crossed the moon. Only one star shone in the ring around it, so she knew it would storm soon.

Stupid, she thought. The stars were suns like the sun that made her hide in her room during the light; only they were millions and millions of miles away, so far that they couldn't hurt her, just sparkle. Mama said that there was no such thing as God, only the Devil, but when the girl looked at all that was held up there in the heavens, she wondered if Mama was wrong.

The Devil made bad things, like her. And that meant there might be something else that made good things like her mama and the night.

"I should go back in," the girl whispered to something in

the darkness. Then the wind blew the scent of the oncoming rain into her nose and mouth and she knew that she wouldn't crawl back through the dog door and up through the hole into her room. Not before she ran.

Rising to her feet, she flew away from the house in which she had been born, her arms and legs bare, her feet uncovered. The wind turned to fire as it rushed into her lungs. She yelped. The cold air and sweaty heat, the stones and briars, stopped hurting when she ran in the darkness.

Mostly she stayed in the trees, just in case, and she had to be careful of the the trunks, felled trees and branches, but in places there were open stretches of tall grass where she ran faster than anybody in the whole world. She almost left her ugly body, she thought, and nearly sailed up through the cold night to fly like a shooting star across the void.

When her breath ran out, she was far into the woods, standing atop a treeless hill, as close to Heaven as she'd ever get. Nothing of the Devil would ever pass those gates, she knew. With her face turned upward, she spun around and around, so the points of light overhead sealed her inside a shimmering cone that led straight up. Oooooo

The dogs answered her howl from somewhere below. It was going to rain very soon. Three dark shapes raced silently toward her. Four-legged, huge, black, their teeth bright like star fragments. Muscles rippling beneath their fur, they sailed up the hill, like fingers of the same deadly hand. When they were close enough, the leader sprang at her without a whisper of warning.

He struck her shoulder and she fell backward. The other two pounced in unison. Together they tumbled down the incline toward the ring of statues, the night suddenly alive with snarls and thrashing.

"Stop it!" she yelled, as bared fangs nipped at her dress and jaws closed on her arms and hands, though without drawing blood. Their rough tongues flashed all over the exposed flesh of her legs and arms. She sat up and pushed at their muzzles.

"Ahriman! Apollyon! Down, down!"

The two obeyed; the third did not.

"Lucifer!"

Lucifer continued his mock snapping. One of his gleaming teeth snagged the rough material that covered her head and jerked it free with a tearing sound.

"Stop." The girl's tone had changed and Lucifer halted instantly. She batted his nose sharply. Whining, he backed away.

She felt along the edge of the hood with her fingers, and then touched her dress. She found the tear near the shoulder where the hood should have fastened tightly. The buttonhole Mama had so painstakingly sewn in, was ripped completely through. Its button hung useless and the chill air wriggled like ice water between her hood and dress. She undid the others.

Lucifer wailed—a high keening—as if he understood. The girl whimpered in reply and peered out from under the hood, not daring to pull it away completely.

A roaring noise came from the road close by, and light arced through the tops of trees down below. The four of them listened. A car. It was sputtering—stopping. The engine sounds died, the halo of light stood still.

Cars hardly ever came here. She had to go to it, even

though Mama was sure to find out. She would hide, no one would see her. They could hunt for things. Maybe there would be parts she could take.

"Come on," she said to the dogs, and fought back the painful awareness that she was going to be bad again. How could she resist it. She pulled the hood back, off, so that it dangled against her neck, and together they raced toward the road, half a mile away, snarling in their throats as they ran.

ERIC HALLIDAY rounded the bend and spotted the car that had passed him three miles back. This was the first sign of life since it had roared by.

The air was cold as hell, his shins hurt, and the backpack had gained fifteen pounds in the last hour, but he couldn't resist the grin that spread across his face when he saw the car was disabled: pulled over to the side, hood raised, a flashlight glancing around the engine block. He stepped onto the shoulder so he wouldn't be easily heard. A few strides brought him even with the car's Florida plates and he saw, bent over the exposed engine, a woman's backside.

She hadn't any idea she wasn't alone, this small woman with reddish blonde hair pulled back in a ponytail like his. She didn't look more than twenty, judging from the hardness of her rump, a well-preserved twenty-five at most. The light flitted about as she excoriated the car with some of the worst language he had ever heard, the diatribe delivered in a New Jersey accent.

"It's your magneto, most likely," he said.

The woman jerked erect, sucking air as she nearly cracked

her head on the upraised hood. The flashlight danced in his face. Shading his eyes, he saw she held a small pistol.

"Who in the hell are you?" she snapped.

The gun so startled him that he nearly gave his real name: "Eric Ha—Abbott. Eric Abbott."

"Where did you come from?""

Damn, she sounded wired enough to put a bullet down his throat if he didn't watch it. "You passed me, back there. About two or three miles."

"Oh." She looked back at the naked engine. The beam of the flashlight swayed toward it, then back into his face. "You know anything about this shit?"

Eric Halliday shielded his eyes with his already upraised hands and gave the car a quick glance. "Not a damned thing."

"Shit. Neither do I." She sighed and shook her head, but the gun remained on him. "What about . . . whatever it was you said—the magneto?"

"It was a joke. Lighten the moment . . . you know?"

"Well, what do we do now?"

"We can tramp along together, I suppose. But I don't really feel all that welcome with the light and the gun in my face. You know what I mean?"

"I'm not leaving this car," she said flatly.

"Okay. Then you can wait until somebody comes along." Florida plates, he thought, and decided to rattle her cage. "Haven't seen another car in two hours though. The next one by here will probably be a county deputy making the morning rounds. He'll be glad to help."

"Damn," she hissed. "I guess I could rent another one."

"Not unless you're a lot older than you look. Automobile

rentals don't take you for human unless you're twenty-five and possessed of active credit cards. Besides, nothing will be open for another nine hours or so."

"Goddamn," she said, in a slow sigh.

"If we were back on 75, we could thumb up the coast. If you've got ready cash, I believe I could swing another rental that would get you back to New Jersey."

"Oh yeah?"

"Yeah. I've got all types of credit cards. And with a shave I can pass."

"You're kind of a free-association talker, aren't you?"

"Sure. Why not. I don't have a trunkload of goodies to worry about."

Her eyes widened; the gun rose higher on his torso. "What do you know?"

Satisfied, Eric Halliday gave her a wink. "Young lady, I've made the mule train from Miami to the Big Apple a few times on my own. For, say, five hundred dollars and the holstering of that weapon, I'll give you the benefit of my dignified demeanor in some rent-a-car office and my companionship on the road outta here."

For a long moment the young woman considered her options, and several times scanned the road in both directions. Then, with a little cough, she slipped the gun in her jacket pocket.

"Charlene Baird," she said, raising her hand in acknowledgment. "Call me Charlie."

"Hi."

"Do me a favor."

"Yeah?"

"Help me carry my luggage."

Halliday grinned. "Pleasure, ma'am."

CHARLENE BAIRD was a first-time dope runner, which was why she was so careless as to take on a perfect stranger on an empty Georgia road in the middle of the night. She'd gotten off at the Duncan County exit just to fuel up somewhere, but then got lost. Funny how things come blindly together, Halliday thought.

Charlene said, "I'm glad I met you, instead of somebody who would clop me over the head and take my stuff."

They had walked less than a mile at the most and already she was on her third cigarette.

She said, "I'm only going to do this once, you know? One time, one gigantic score and, bam! I'm set for life."

You'll probably be raped, slit, and dumped in the Hudson by your wholesaler up there, babe, he thought. How much was the stuff worth that they were carrying in the three suitcases. He tried to calculate their weight and value.

She said, "I wouldn't have thought to shove the son of a bitching car off the road if you hadn't brought it up. Thanks."

"No extra charge," he said. Eric Halliday might live off of women but he wasn't a killer or dope dealer. Her emergency cash would be enough. "Are you sure this is the way to the interstate?"

Charlene gave him a look. "You don't know?"

"Do I sound like I'm from this jerkwater place."

They stopped and dropped their bags and pack. She smiled, he smiled; they began to laugh. The laughter lasted only until the rain began.

"Oh God, oh damn!" Charlene gasped as fat drops hit, the icy wetness plastering the clothes to her flesh in seconds. "God, don't get the stuff wet!"

The bottom dropped out of the sky. It was suddenly infinitely colder. They were drenched, water dripping from their chins.

"Shit," Eric exclaimed. "What do you want me to do, sit on the friggin' things?"

He took up two of the bags and his backpack; she shouldered one. There was no moon anymore, just roiling clouds.

"The car!" she shrieked. "Let's get back to it and wait this out."

"No," he shouted, over the noise of the rain. "Too far. Get off the road—under the trees. Maybe it'll blow over."

He hopped over the rapidly filling ditch, and Charlene followed, the flashlight out and gleaming.

The pines were pressed close together, forcing them to grow tall and slender, like telephone poles. They were tightly clumped but their branches didn't shield very much. So the two ran deeper into the forest, the faint yellow line of the highway quickly vanishing.

Great, Eric cursed to himself, the only thing worse than being lost on a road is being lost without one. Charlie, he guessed, from the wildly swinging beam of her flashlight, was coming to the same conclusion. The light glanced off something.

"Wait!" he said loudly, over the pelting rain. "What was that?"

"What?" she yelled, close to her emotional edge.

"Over there." He took her wrist and turned it. "Over there, back to your right."

The light fell on a structure—a barn. Old, skewed, steel gray—or maybe green—with three sides on the ground and the crown of the roof oddly angled, the fourth side high off the ground.

"Come on," Eric yelled and charged toward it.

"Are you nuts? The thing will fall on top of us."

"So what. At least that'll be quicker than turning our asses into popsicles out here."

He reached the wall and stooped alongside a gaping hole. Without hesitating, he tossed the two suitcases in ahead of him and scrambled after. She followed, reluctantly but quickly.

"I hate this. Jesus, I hate this!" she squawked. Something scurried by. "I think this room is already taken."

But it was dry. She shoved her bag next to the others and swung the light around. No ghouls, snakes, or whiskey stills, and it was surprisingly spacious—empty.

"I'm freezing to death," she said, her teeth chattering, ribs quaking.

"Start a fire," he said.

"How?" she said.

"How do you light your cigarettes?"

She grinned, embarrassed. "Oh yeah."

He scraped some wood and hay into a pile so they wouldn't send the whole place up and Charlene ignited it. She wrinkled her nose at the overpowering stink of rotting, burning wood and petrified animal droppings.

HER SKIN puckered into tight bumps in the freezing rain. She stopped and held up her arms, baying. The dogs howled, she with them, her throat glistening.

Then they took up their run. They were joined by two hounds from the Wiley farm some miles across the ridgeline. Together they raced to the west, tracking the odors of the car. There were times when her body's excitement cut off her mind and she was more like them than herself, strange free moments. Her mama's voice chastised her. Tonight she didn't care. The Devil was her father, her mother had said.

The dogs fell silent; she did, too. They kept moving. She wished she could hear the things the dogs heard. She smelled smoke. And then she smelled them.

''ARE WE gonna spend the whole damned night in here?'' Charlene sighed. Though the fire felt a lot better than would the icy rain peppering the collapsed barn.

"You can go anytime," Eric replied and shrugged. "'Course you'll have to carry your own shit, or leave it behind, 'cause I'm not moving until the weather lets up. On the upside, though, I'll only charge you half of the contracted five hundred for services rendered up till now."

Charlene frowned. Her first experience in big-time crime wasn't turning out the way she'd envisioned. "Don't forget that I've got the gun, smartass."

"How far do you think I could carry two suitcases with a bullet in my back, Charlie?" He snickered, arms tight across his chest, trying to warm up.

She exhaled heavily. "Shit."

A dog howled. Their eyes locked.

"Christ, are they looking for us?" she gasped.

He had momentarily thought the same thing but covered his reaction with a short laugh. "At night? In the rain? Don't worry. No self-respecting bloodhound would allow himself to be dragged out on a night like this. And even if they were, they'd never be able to follow our trail on a paved road in this downpour."

"But that sounded so close."

"Farm dogs," he said, nudging the fire with his toe. "You're in the country, not tripping down the streets of Hoboken." The howling erupted again; more than one this time. "Or maybe it's a feral pack."

"Feral?"

"Wild. Abandoned dogs gone back to the basics."

"There are wild dogs out there?" Her eyes were white.

"Hey, you've got the gun," he reminded her. "Chill out."

An enraged cry broke over the howl of the dogs.

"That was no farm hound," Charlene said.

Eric shifted his weight from his haunches to his knees and stared out into the darkness beyond the hole. Their small fire didn't cast much light. "Sounded like . . . ."

"Maybe those stupid dogs are after somebody."

He didn't want to consider such a possibility. "Nah."

"You gotta go look."

"Forget it."

"Eric!"

Then he had an idea. "You're the one with the hardware," he said.

"Hey, man. I don't want to be the second course. Here," she said.

"No."

"No, really. Here."

With seeming reluctance, he accepted the pistol. Nine millimeter, fifteen rounds. Not bad, he thought, feeling safer. It wasn't the gun she had waved at him earlier; that was a smaller caliber. But what the heck, now he had a vote, too. "Okay. Give me the goddamned flashlight."

Charlene handed it over and watched Eric ease cautiously out the jagged hole. His footfalls receded into the general din of the downpour. She waited, feeling truly alone. It was taking longer than she had expected. She edged closer to the fire. As the minutes passed, the solace of the collective weight of one hundred, fifty high-grade pounds yielded to a tremulous panic. How in the name of heaven had she wound up here? Lost in Yokel Land without a car, paired off with a cool-eyed fugitive from the 60s, a couple of body degrees above hypothermia. Damn, Paulie, how did I let you talk me into this?

Smoke was building up in the tippy roof above her. No problem, she thought. It was burning warm and clean, and she added a few more scraps of wood, carefully stomping out the sparks that threatened the hay and duff Eric had scraped away to make a rough circle. It was heating up, actually; she was drying out. She pulled the damp cigarettes from the pack and spread them atop her pantleg so that they could soak up the radiant heat faster. This wasn't bad at all, but she wished he would hurry the hell back.

Then she heard footsteps, running. If he hadn't split on her yet, he was doing it now. Charlene scrambled to her feet, dumping precious cigarettes every which way.

"Eric, goddamn it. Eric!"

She ran to the opening in the wall and thrust her face into the rain, which slapped away in an instant all the warmth her body had managed to husband. She scampered outside.

"Eric."

Then he was on her, bent over, stumbling out of the darkness, terrified, rigid with panic, right into the side of the barn, full tilt. The rotting structure wobbled like a drum but held together. Eric was on his butt on the forest floor.

"Eric!" she screamed. "What's wrong?"

He was too terrified. He leaped up to grasp her shoulders. "Give me your gun."

"But what's happening? Where's yours?"

"Give me the gun, you stupid slut!" He clawed at the pockets of her coat.

"Are you crazy? What's the matter with you?" Charlene shouted. A desperate strength surged through her body but she couldn't break loose from the overwhelmed man, and they fell back together, into the barn.

Eric's hand found the gun and ripped her coat open to get it.

"Okay, okay," she gasped, his wild eyes freezing her heart.

"I got to get out. I can't—I can't—"

He spun about and leapt for the opening. Charlene grabbed a suitcase.

"Wait! Help me!"

Something dead and white had Eric's hair and face. Charlene shrieked, Eric's wail echoing hers as he vanished through the gap.

"Oh my God." She scrambled to the back of the collapsed room. She had to find a way out, there had to be a way out. Eric screamed. Charlene pounded the back wall, then threw her shoulder against it. The wood shuddered, dust and dirt cascading down on her.

She realized it was quiet, only the rain and the crackling fire, and her own locomotive breathing.

Something round flew in, like a ball, and bounced across the floor and onto the fire, snuffing it out.

"No, no."

Darkness filled the barn like fluid. Charlie's throat clenched shut. There had been a soft sound, she realized. Something had come into the rotted barn, was there in the dark, with her. She slowly eased down to her hands and knees, fighting the panic. Easy, she thought. Easy. She had played this game with her brothers, in the dark. Commandos. Barely breathing, she crawled toward where she thought the hole was, feeling her way across the dirt floor. Through the animal spoors, hay, rotted wood dust. The ground was warmer. She was near the fire. Her hand touched something large. The ball, she thought, until she felt the brow and the bridge of the nose.

THEY RAN and ran, the rain cold and sweet on them, their bodies shiny and strong. The dogs suddenly stopped. They skidded in the red-colored mud, and she fell, trying to stop with them.

The dogs' ears stood straight up. She knew they were listening to a sound she couldn't hear—the whistle. And then they were gone, away through the darkness, leaving her alone. She needed more time, and more rain to wash her and her dress, but the rain was letting up, too.

"Rain," she cried. The rain grew lighter. She could run until the sun came up but she could never get away, she knew. She could hide in the caves until the roots of the grass and trees grew down and wrapped her up like the winter cocoons that tasted so good on her tongue, but Mama would find her eventually. She always found her. Mama could see the truth, even through her hood.

Nervously, she threw herself into a puddle. Water splashed up her nostrils, burning and making her sneeze, but her hands were busy wiping and kneading her dress to get the terrible stains out before Mama could see.

"MaryAnn!"

She gasped. She thought the whimpering sound that answered had come from one of the dogs, but it was from her.

"MaryAnn, damn you. Get back here. Now!"

Her lip trembled. "Yes, Mama," she whispered, and pulled the hood back over her head.

Getting to her feet, she waded out of the pooling water and stumbled back along the path to the house, buttoning as she went. The gas lantern her mother held cut the darkness. The look in the woman's eyes emptied her somehow. She felt hollow. When her mother could see her too, her eyes got even colder.

"Where have you been?"

"I . . . I was outside."

The rubber loop swung slowly at her mother's side. It struck out at the girl and her vision exploded in light and agony. She dropped to her knees with a moan.

"Get in the house. Get in your room." The awful belt came down on her head, her shoulders and back, like lightning. The girl scrambled on hands and knees through the doorway, pleading and growling.

"Mama! Please. I'm sorry, please!"

But the rubber belt continued to snap, biting through the cloth and into her flesh.

"What else did you do? Tell me, all of it."

The girl crawled through the blackness of the house, and every snap of the belt seemed to shoot its pain directly into her brain in rainbow lights.

"Answer me!"

"I was bad, Mama. Please don't hit me."

She had reached the room. The door was open and unlocked from when her mother had looked inside to find her gone. The girl rushed in and fell on the crude bed. Mama followed. The rubber strap struck the wall above her with a horrible whack.

"Show me where you got out." Her mother raised the lantern high to light the corner. "Where?"

"Under the table. The boards came up. I went through the bottom of the house," the girl said, still hiding her face from the strap.

Her mother sighed. "You crawled through the floor into the dog pen and through their door, on your hands and knees, like a *damned animal!* What am I supposed to do, MaryAnn? Tell me! How am I supposed to treat you if you keep acting like a beast? Do you want to live with the dogs?"

The girl's entire body trembled. "No, ma'am. I want to stay with you, Mama, always I do."

For the briefest instant the woman's face softened with what might have been sadness, or maybe pity.

"Tell," she said. "All of it, MaryAnn. Did you do anything? Anything?"

The girl whimpered softly into the bed, hunched on her knees into a ball.

"MaryAnn."

"Yes, Mama. I did. I'm sorry. I couldn't help myself. I really—"

Her voice broke with a shriek of pain as the strap lashed her hips, her thighs. The woman swung with all her might, grunting at the effort.

"Don't"—whack—"*ever*"—whack—"do"—whack—"that"—whack—"again."

She panted, the girl wailed. Recovering her breath, the woman resumed her task.

"You will *never*"—whack—"leave this room"—whack—"without me."

The rubber strap whipped down hard three times in quick succession. Even as she yelped and writhed in terrible, searing pain, the girl knew her mother was tiring. The rubber whistled softly again. *Whack!*

"Do you understand?"

"Yes, Mama. Yes, yes. Oh, please don't. Oh, Mama, don't hurt me more. Please."

The woman stood over her fifteen year old daughter, wheezing loudly. The girl stopped moving and stayed curled in a ball. No matter how much it hurt, she knew it was better not to cry out or writhe, or the blows just got harder. She tried not to move, not to shake. When her mother could speak again, she said, "Take off your clothes."

"M-ma'am?"

"Your clothes, take them off. You can't sleep in that."

The girl fumbled with the buttons of her dress, then stepped out of it, naked except for the hood.

"That too."

The girl's hands fluttered to the edge of the covering. "Mama?" she said, plaintively.

"It's got to be cleaned."

"Okay." Her voice sounded small and hopeless. "Please don't look, Mama."

"Just give it to me," the woman said in an exhausted tone, but turned sideways, half compliant.

The girl whipped off the hood and crawled beneath the sheets on her bed, her eyes to the wall, even the touch of the sheet searing her flesh where the rubber had bitten. The woman gathered up the soiled dress. The belt had cut through in places across the back.

"Mama." It was a whisper.

"What?"

"I'm real sorry." The words were almost lost in the bedding pressed against her lip. "I didn't mean to do bad. I was just playing."

"Playing what, MaryAnn?"

"God."

The woman stepped out of the windowless room, taking the light with her. She closed the heavy door and bolted it, then leaned against it with great weariness. An infinitely woeful smile animated her face momentarily.

"MaryAnn and God," she said to herself in a whisper.

2

THE SUN was dazzling; it had raised the temperature into the seventies by afternoon. The first of real spring days to come.

Now this is what the South should be like, Lola Aragon thought, as she stood before the picture window of her office. Back in New York there was probably an inch of sleet in the streets. Friday. She had been in Sturgis, Georgia, exactly one week.

"Nice, isn't it?" said Claudette Williams, coming in.

Lola turned from the window, smiling. "If you could eat sunshine, I'd gain ten pounds."

"You could do twenty and not have to worry," Claudette replied enviously.

Lola colored. She was tall, fit, an able educator, a not bad gymnast and terribly self-conscious in some ways. Claudette paused at the window.

"I only wish this would last," she said. "I hate winter."

"You mean it gets cold here? I thought it was always warm."

"Hey, this isn't Rio de Janeiro. We had twelve inches of snow in January. And I'd bet we get some frigid days before summer."

Lola eased into the high-backed swivel chair at her desk and glanced at the clock. "When is that patrol car going to get here."

Claudette smiled. "Relax, Dr. Aragon. You're in the South now, the land of gentility, Southern charm and laid back time concepts."

"Yes, but I've got two schools to check today, and where are they?"

"Y'all 'll have a great time," Claudette teased, glancing at her watch. "They'll be here any second. Besides . . ."

"Besides what?"

Claudette feigned a rapturous expression. "Jimmy and Ross are worth the wait."

"Are those the officers?"

"Deputies Lowell and Walker, yes'm."

Lola exhaled, her cheeks puffed, and riffled through a stack of papers on her desk. She's nervous Claudette thought, new-job nerves. Understandably so. Claudette had peeked in her personnel file. The lady was accomplished: Columbia Teachers College, Assistant Director of the Bank Street School, Family Court Advisor for Bronx County. Twenty-nine and about to assume the running of the county's educational services administration. A fast-tongued Latina with a typical Yankee veneer of assumed superiority. Compensating for her age maybe. Still, nice enough. She would ease into her new life if she stayed around long enough.

"Here they come," Claudette announced. The car had pulled up out front.

"Good," Lola said, without looking up from the paperwork she'd been perusing.

"Jimmy Lowell sure is good looking, what with all that height and those Clint Eastwood moves. I think he's half convinced he's Dirty Harry. Anyway, he's married. But Ross . . . . Hey, he's trying to grow a beard again. I hope Sheriff Malone lets him keep it when he gets back from Atlanta."

"What's the sheriff got to do with this deputy's beard?" Lola asked, and wondered why she had.

"It's against regulations. Isn't it up North?"

"No," Lola said. "I don't believe so."

"Is down here." Claudette fell silent. She was was watching the deputies saunter.

Lola Aragon exhaled again, trying not to be too much of a Yankee. Stop ticking, she told herself. What was the matter with her foot? She massaged her foot and groaned.

"Something wrong?" Claudette said.

"Cramp in my foot."

"Turn your shoes upside down before turning in tonight."

"What?" Lola said, with an incredulous look.

"An old remedy. Works, too." Claudette smiled.

"Thanks for the medical advice."

"Are you married, Dr. Aragon?" Claudette knew the answer, but it would have been impolite to have the information without Lola Aragon's imparting it.

"Divorced. Recently divorced."

"You know about getting back on the horse, I guess," Claudette drawled. "Men and horses aren't all that different, I find."

"Some are more like jackasses," said Lola.

DEPUTY LOWELL was at least six-foot-three, and very lean and leathery. The uniform was razor-creased, the eyes invisible behind silvered aviator sunglasses. He had "I'm-one-tough-stud" stamped all over him. Clean Harry, she thought.

Ross Walker was six feet tall but dwarfed by his partner. Bearded, no sunglasses, friendly eyes. After cursory introductions, he opened the back door of the brown and yellow police cruiser for her.

"So," he said, "you're the whiz kid from New York who's come down to redesign and revitalize the Duncan County educational system."

"I wouldn't put it that way," she said. "The school system is functioning nicely enough, according to the test scores. Comfortably above the national average."

He smiled amid the beard. "Well, it turned me out into the world, but I guess every system is allowed the occasional glitch."

The conversation ended there as she got in. It was a police car, and even in the slow and easy South, it came equipped with a protective partition separating the front and back seats. This one was plastic, with tiny air holes. So while the deputies carried on in muffled tones up front, she was left to her thoughts in back. There weren't any interior door handles, either, she noted.

Lola watched the town roll by. Sturgis was not so small or rustic as she had envisioned it, while furiously packing for this impulsive migration south. (She was decisive, if she was anything.) She had expected to find, at best, a Mayberry R.F.D., and at its worst a Tennessee Williams' Hollywood nightmare of a white-trash metropolis. In fact, it was an industrial city of 25,000 hard working citizens. Through some fluke she did not understand, the modern carpet industry had been launched in its vicinity at the turn of the century, and local restaurants displayed photographs from that era of roadside stands covered with handcrafted throwrugs. After the Second World War, factories blossomed and full rugs were mass produced; Sturgis was a boom town. By the mid-sixties, with some legitimacy, it pronounced itself the Carpet Capital of the World. It wasn't a shady southern hamlet by any means, but it still had a certain visual appeal.

Factories whizzed by, and strips of wholesale outlets and retailers. Still, for all the manufacturing that had gone on here for nearly a century, Sturgis wasn't at all like the decaying textile-mill towns she had seen in the Northeast. And the surrounding countryside retained its rural integrity—dairy herds, farms, and long stretches of isolated woodlands—that kept Sturgis from evolving into a stark city, like Cleveland or Pittsburgh.

The countryside outside town was impressive. Although still bleak with winter-gray vegetation, there were plenty of evergreens and moody forests dotted with buds. The Appalachian range ended somewhere around here, she knew, from having studied the state map one evening, but all she could make out were flat areas and hills, gentle slopes and sharp rises.

Yes, the people did talk funny, and, yes, there was suspicion in many of the faces she encountered. Her accent and mannerisms, after all, were foreign, nor could one deny the social stratification along racial lines. But it wasn't *Deliverance,* or even Dogpatch USA. She could live down here for a while, live and regroup. At least until she had recovered from the acidic effects of her recently jettisoned spouse. After that . . . she had her whole life ahead of her.

The sign, as they turned off the highway, said Northview High School. The driveway wasn't long. The car eased to a stop and her escorts got out. She didn't—couldn't. No door handles.

Deputy Lowell busied himself with extracting the lecture material from the trunk; Deputy Walker meantime was being monopolized by some ebullient functionary carrying on a rapid-fire monologue as they walked toward the building.

"Oh, great," Lola sighed. She rapped on the window sharply. Ross Walker stopped dead. At least he had keen ears. With a half-embarrassed grin, he quickly returned and opened the door for her.

"Sorry about that, Dr. Aragon. A case of crossed wires," he said, with a nod toward Lowell.

She gave him a cold look and ignored the proffered hand as she got out. Walker introduced her to Porter Kolda, the principal, and they moved together toward the auditorium. Mr. Kolda shook her hand, gave her the once over, and re-marked on her New York accent. He was twice her age, sandy-haired and anxious. He would be even more anxious when she was announced next week as the new county director of education and his, and the other three principals', boss.

"You're here to help with the lecture?" he said.

"To monitor it, actually."

"Dr. Aragon," said Deputy Walker, "has been hired to show us country folk how to clog dance through the back door into the twenty-first century."

Lola forced a smile. You certainly are playing up the comic defensiveness, buddy, she thought. Just ingratiating banter or a sign of real cultural jealousy?

Inside, the auditorium was packed with students. Some of the girls wore pants, she noticed; the boys wore sweatshirts and sweaters. Hairstyles ranged from quite short among some of the girls to moderately long for a portion of the boys, but there were no ponytails, and neither sex was permitted to experiment with outrageous cuts or colors. In Duncan County classrooms, she had been told during her interview, the fourth "R" referred to Respectability.

About two-thirds appeared to be white Anglo Saxon Protestants, one-fifth blacks, and there seemed to be a surprising number of Hispanics and Asians. Without preamble, the first officer launched into his pitch. It couldn't have been further from the cornsilk-behind-the-woodshed chiding that she had expected. He reeled off the nasty facts about pot, dust, crack, smack, even designer drugs and alcohol. James Lowell knew his stuff. He was forceful and blunt as he narrated the slide show of overdosed victims, syringe-sharing AIDS patients, druggies nodding out, wired crackheads in living color, and the totalled victims of impaired drivers, the needlessly abused victims of drugged-out thieves, and family members assaulted by relatives who had had too much or too little of their private poisons coursing through their veins. His delivery verged on hectoring at times, but he was damned effective she thought.

So was Ross Walker, in his own fashion. Deputy Walker had no slides, no samples, no props. In a quiet, even tone he simply recounted one case. It involved a child, a little boy of three whose parents started innocently with a "safe" drug and graduated to harder stuff. Neglect and abuse followed. Four times the child had been removed from his home by the County Child and Spouse Service, and each time his parents succeeded in regaining custody. The fifth time they failed. Eighteen days short of his fourth birthday, Deputy Walker had rushed the boy to the hospital in the front seat of his police car.

"He died with his head on my thigh, me doin' ninety on Shelby Road. I couldn't even hold his hand."

The hall was silent, except for the low weeping of some of the girls. Ross Walker cleared his throat.

"I couldn't cry for him on that day, and I haven't been able to since. All I feel is an incredible hatred for those two addicts. I'm not going to stand here and tell you what's right or wrong. But you've got to know that illegal drugs, or legal alcohol, they are not your private business. They affect everyone you affect."

Lola was impressed by the impact on the high schoolers. The stylish reserve and overt disparagement she had come to expect from New York kids lolling through dope lectures, and which she'd mildly detected during Jimmy Lowell's first-half, seemed totally absent now. These laid-back lawmen had really gotten through to the youngsters.

A question-and-answer session followed. The questioning was lively but, for the most part, shallow and standard. Lowell fielded most of them (still wearing mirrored glasses and deputy's cap). Walker seemed content with the arrangement. They were just wrapping up when a big husky kid, with deep-set eyes and brown hair, rose up and raised his hand. The clothes were good, the look wasn't. She had seen the same cold, self-important expression in plenty of teenagers' faces. No matter the sex or shade, the look meant trouble.

Lowell recognized the boy with a nod.

"My question's for the other cop," the boy said, "the one who found the dead kid."

Walker paced the apron of the stage, hands in his pockets. "Yes."

"Those two—the parents? Why didn't you lynch 'em? Or would hangin' fresh meat out to cure like that have violated some health department regulation?"

Most were stunned by the incredibly ugly remark. Kids gasped, a few jeered. A ring of lackeys laughed and applauded the boy. So much for Southern civility, Lola thought, and watched Ross Walker to see how he'd respond. He didn't. Lowell leaned over the microphone.

"Mister, you need to have your butt kicked hard enough to shake your brains into shape."

The audience cheered; the boy, still standing, recoiled in mock horror, his compatriots hooting. Principal Kolda stepped up to the mike. "Fenton Lindsey will report to my office immediately following the assembly." He thanked the officers profusely and dismissed the student body.

Lowell carried the demonstration kit, leading the way back to the car. In the parking lot, Walker finally extricated himself from the principal with a modicum of tact.

"Ready to go, Dr. Aragon?" he said.

"Why don't you call me Lola, Deputy?"

He smiled. "'Whatever Lola Wants.'"

"Ah, a man who knows his show tunes."

"Call me Ross."

"Okay, Ross. You know, I'm almost convinced you really meant what you were saying in there."

He shook his head slightly. "Damn Yankees."

"What?" she said, surprised.

He opened the back door of the police car for her and stood aside. "*Damn Yankees,*" he said, "the show the song's from," and doffed his cap as she got in.

SEATED ACROSS from Principal Kolda and listening to the dressing down for his remarks in the assembly, Fenton Lindsey coolly drew a rolled joint from his gym bag and lit up.

Kolda's lips froze and his eyes seemed to double in size. When he was able to speak, his voice was barely a raw whisper.

"What in God's name are you doing?"

Fenton exhaled. I'm waiting for June, he thought, so I can leave this shithole in the cold, dead past. What do you think, you dumb jerk. He said, "Just relaxing through the rough spots, Boss."

"Put that thing *out.*"

"You want a toke?"

"Put it out!"

The boy took a long pull and held it while he stubbed the end in an ashtray on the principal's cherry wood desk, then tucked the remains back into the bag. "You really . . ." he said in a high, thin voice as he exhaled. "You really ought . . . to try it, man. Keeps the blood pressure down. Great for you if you're terminal, too."

Kolda leaned forward, elbows on the immaculate desktop, his expression one of total disbelief and anger. "How can you sit through what you heard from those two men and still put that foul crap in yourself?"

Fenton shrugged. This was getting old. It was Friday, the weather was so great that the nightlife would be starting long before dark, and this gas-passing monkey couldn't get past his smoking habit. Come on, asshole, take your cut or clear off the plate.

"I saw *Jaws*," he said, "but I still eat fish."

"I won't have that insolent tone used in my office, Mr. Lindsey."

Fenton smirked. He leaned forward onto the desktop, too. "Listen, Kolda. We both know that you're not going to hit me, because I'll break your back. We also know that you're not going to suspend me or do anything else to mess up my grades, because my old man will go nuts and his bank just might call in a few outstanding loans. Right?"

Kolda's face lost all trace of shock. He was now a study in impotent rage.

Fenton said, "Oh, and I don't feel like doing any detention. Now, give me the bottom line so I can get the hell out of this place for a couple of days."

I T W A S barely half past two and all six had cut their last classes: Fenton Lindsey and five of his friends and stooges tooling around the sticks in the black van that he used for what he called cattle drives—meandering around the back-roads with a group of sharps, looking for diversion. The interior was hazy with sweet, tangy smoke.

Gail Parker was aghast. "You *really* lit up right there, in his office? In front of his face?"

Fenton savored the toke and the moment. "Damn straight. Toked it right down to my teeth. The old bastard's eyeballs liked to 've popped right out of his skull."

"All right!" laughed Kimball Johnson, known—at his insistence—as KJ. He stroked Deirdre Bennett's arm. "You shoulda took a camera in there and made a video of it."

The van careened down the empty road as wildly as if no one were at the wheel. There seemed to be no trace of human habitation this deep into the countryside, other than the paved two-lane road. The grabassing and lying continued for some time, until Gail Parker said, "Tell me something, Fen."

"For you, no charge, baby."

"Why the hell are we driving out here in the middle of the great Georgia wastelands? I'm not dressed for exploring new continents."

Kimball Johnson turned from the steering wheel to answer, and the van missed a nosedive into the ditch by half a foot. "Hey," he said, "tell me where to go and we'll go, all right? You guys just said to get into the country."

"You're doing fine, KJ," Fenton said. He was real mellow and the coming night would be a good one. "Just keep cruising."

In the distance a black mailbox came into view, the only thing breaking the monotony of the roadbed. It sat next to a largely overgrown turnoff that ran through a set of large gates and a fence and disappeared into the forested slope behind the chainlinks. Kimball Johnson pulled the van off the road just beyond it.

"What's the matter, man? Butt itch?" said Alex Schneider, a sixteen year old who was included in the group only because he consistently scored prime dope.

Johnson slipped out of the driver's seat, shaking his head. "Pit stop," he said and got out of the van, heading for the woods.

"Oh, great," muttered Gail. "There goes twenty minutes."

In the front passenger seat, Roger Casey rolled down the window and laid his arm across the sill, his chin atop that. He stared out through his thick glasses, at nothing Fenton could find of interest since there was nothing out there but the mailbox, fence, gate, the rutted driveway, and about a billion goddamned trees.

Of all his entourage, Fenton was the least comfortable with Casey. A runty, nearsighted geek on the outside, the inside of Roger Casey was deeply strange in ways that Fenton continually found shocking, which was something for someone who had thought himself acquainted with every non-lethal kick available to a rich eighteen year old in the Free World. Casey was wired weird.

"What's on your mind, Slick," Fenton said in a casual tone.

"I'm wondering what she looks like now," Roger Casey said, still staring out. "She must be almost sixteen."

"Yeah?" said Alex Schneider. "Who?" Ever anxious to prove he was as down and dirty as any of them. "We need some fresh blood in this crowd."

Gail laughed. "Like it would do *you* any good, Jail Bait."

At seventeen, Roger Casey was still smaller and lighter than Alex, but no one ever treated him with that kind of disrespect. Not given the bizarre stunts he'd been known to pull.

"Who?" Fenton said.

"The Spook." Casey nodded toward the slopes. "This is where she lives."

"Shit," whispered Gail.

"Where's KJ," Deirdre said, sounding worried.

Alex Schneider snorted. "Get off it, man. There ain't no such thing. It's a myth."

Roger Casey shook his head slowly. "Brotherly love is a myth, the New Wave's a myth. So's your chances of getting laid. But the Spook's real, and she lives right over . . . there." He pointed.

The door snapped open, sounding like a drum rim shot. Everyone, except Casey, jumped.

"Jesus Christ, KJ," Gail whined. "You almost made me swallow my tongue!"

The boy looked confused. "What's up?"

"Shut up, KJ," Fenton said. "How do you know she lives out here, Slick?"

"See the mailbox? M. Nelson. That's her old lady."

"The family name is Nelson?" Deirdre said, sounding none too happy about it. Everyone looked over at her, as if surprised to see her along. Actually, no one was sure how she'd come to be in the group. She didn't do dope and she didn't chugalug. But she did put out for Fenton without charging him for it.

"Yes. Nelson," Casey said. "And I don't mean Ozzie and Harriet."

"Who what?" KJ asked, a step behind as usual.

"The Spook," Fenton said. "Now shut your mouth and let the man talk."

"Damn, she ain't real," Kimball Johnson muttered.

"The few folks who live in this part of the county would disagree," Casey said. "They say she comes out 'in the stillness of the night,' as it were. A slim, white wraith. Transparent, with hair completely gray. Usually she stays on her side of the road, back up in there. Whenever they see her across the way, though, the locals are left poorer in the way of livestock. Some even claim that drifters, and assorted losers unlikely to be missed, don't often make it past this point in the road when the Spook is about."

"Sounds unlikely," Gail said, trying for a reasoned tone.

Casey smiled. "MaryAnn Nelson. No middle name. Born at the Solstice—June twenty-first. Mother: Nedra Muriel Nelson. No father of record. Birth certificate signed and filed by Joseph Endicott, M.D."

"Dr. Endicott," Deirdre gasped, the prominent name suddenly making the rest credible.

"And that, my friends, is the extent of the official documentation of the life of the unfortunate MaryAnn Nelson. Everything else has been derived from alleged sightings by alleged eyewitnesses, and stories told by the locals on windy evenings."

"Stories," Gail repeated. "That's probably all they are, Roger Casey. Like the tall tales the seniors told about her when we were sophomores. Remember? Turned out to be pure bullshit. They never came anywhere near seein' her. A bunch of Halloween crap."

"Up at the Nelsons', every night is Halloween." Casey turned away from the window; he looked right at her. "Some of the local people claim old lady Nelson is every bit as terrifying as her fabled daughter."

"We should get our chance to find out soon enough," Gail said, and pointed up the dirt track. "Here she comes."

Slowly, arduously, came a strange looking contraption—a combination tricycle and pedal driven golf cart—powered by a tall, sinewy woman. The vehicle had two tall rear wheels, and a smaller one in front which acted as a steering column. An overhead canopy shielded the rider and any passengers. In the rear were two bucket seats and a trunk-like box. The wheels, they now saw, were made of hard rubber, and all badly chipped. Her sweater was as black and dirty as the tires, the blue jeans worn nearly gray with age and washings.

"Hey," Alex exclaimed, "I've seen her riding around town. Her and that stupid looking bicycle. I always thought her name was Cycle Sue."

Fenton squinted to see her better. The woman pumping the contraption down the hill looked hard and unkempt, her gray hair billowing back from under the wide-brimmed straw hat. He guessed she might be fifty or sixty; it was hard to tell from her weathered, resentful face. But it was disturbingly obvious that she had once been remarkably attractive, before fate intervened. She looked mean and strong. Hell, he thought, riding that pedal-powered monstrosity would keep anyone in shape.

When she saw them, as she descended the hill, her features became even sterner. Her stare was withering to all but Casey, who actually smiled. He stepped out of the van, onto the roadside. Not to appear candyassed, the other five quickly followed. Nedra Muriel Nelson rolled toward them down the hill without a word. She stopped at the gates, dismounted, unlocked and opened one-half, remounted, rode through, and relocked them. The six youngsters stood in a rough semicircle, watching.

"Good afternoon," Casey said, as she started to board the strange cycle. "Going to town, Miss Nelson?"

She stopped, then turned to stand with hands on hips, and gazed at them. Her eyes seemed to peel the flesh from whomever they fell upon.

"Get off my land."

Casey leaned back against the side panel of the van and crossed his legs at the ankles. "I don't think you own this road out here, ma'am."

Muriel Nelson glared, but that was all she could do, obviously. Accepting the situation, she re-mounted the cycle.

"Are you?" Casey said. "Going to town, I mean."

"What I do is none of your business, boy. I'd advise you and your delinquent friends to move on."

Kimball Johnson laughed. Everyone else stood motionless, watching.

Casey said, very innocently, "Where's the danger, ma'am?"

Muriel Nelson ignored the remark and began pedaling. Casey grinned. "How's the family, Miss Nelson? MaryAnn doing well?"

Muriel Nelson froze. A real reaction; the others smiled. Casey droned on, casually.

"She'll be having her sweet sixteen party in a couple of months, won't she?"

Fenton felt himself tremble, an exciting sensation. It was Roger Casey, his eeriness and unpredictability, the way his words went out like heat-seeking missiles, honing right in on the most vulnerable places. You'd have thought his indiscriminate attacks might have provoked painful retaliation, especially from his peers, but Casey's reputation was formidable. The dude was nuts.

"Have you made up a guest list yet?" Casey said.

"You little piece of shit," she said. "You have no idea, do you? You just can't understand what it might be like."

"I'll bet she's looking real nice by now, huh? How about letting us cruise back to your place so we can take a peek at her?"

"Come on, Roger," Deirdre whispered. "Cut it out!"

Muriel Nelson smiled at them, a scary smile. Her voice surprisingly level, she said, "Maybe I should let you do that. Maybe you need to see her."

"No thanks, Janks," Alex Schneider said, chuckling nervously.

"Well?" Muriel said, looking at Casey.

He nodded, then stepped forward. "Lady, I'll kiss her on the lips—if she's got any."

"Yuck," Gail Parker exclaimed; Kimball Johnson shook his head in disgust and laughed. Fenton stood planted, awed by Roger Casey's nervy assault.

The woman turned back toward the cycle. At first they thought she might be moving it out of the way of the gate: that she'd open it. Instead, she withdrew a long object from beneath a tarp that covered the rearmost seats. When she turned back to them, the thing arced and they stood riveted, suddenly hypnotized by the dark twin holes of a shotgun. It boomed just over their heads, the concussion slamming their ears.

"Son of a bitch!" Alex screamed. He spun about and sprinted for the van, diving inside. Deirdre, Gail, KJ, and even Fenton ran too. Only Casey remained rooted, a pinky massaging one ear.

"Git!" the woman ordered.

Casey shook his head no.

Fenton, cupping his mouth, yelled, "Are you crazy, Slick? Get your ass in here."

"Roger," Deirdre yelled, "come on."

Casey only smiled, in that crazy way of his. Muriel brought the shotgun level with his chest.

"Move or die, bastard."

Casey, in the softest voice, said, "Shoot."

"Jesus Christ!" Alex shouted, and dived for the floor of the van.

The weapon held as steady as the limb of an oak. Even Casey, with his fat-lensed glasses, could see her forefinger go white as it applied pressure to the trigger. His entire body clenched painfully, but he stood in.

She lowered the gun. "You've got balls, kid. You may have the brain of a slug, but you put a lot of grown men to shame."

"We can see her then?" he said. "We'll pay money."

"Not on your life."

Before he could protest, Muriel Nelson tossed the shotgun onto the rear seats and took a long metal tube from her shirt pocket. When she blew on it and they didn't hear any whistle, they immediately suspected what it was. And they were right.

Within seconds, two huge, black Dobermans came racing from amid the trees, and a moment later a third joined them. Reaching the fence, they barked furiously at the strangers and leapt like spring-loaded toys at the tall gate.

"There are more like them, and worse, roaming all over my land. They'll kill you if you take one step inside my property. Your asses will be hamburger."

Awaiting no reply, she resumed her seat and pedaled off, heading east toward Sturgis, some fifteen miles away. The cycle's weight made the start up ponderous, but by the time she was fifty yards down the road, the thing was moving at a brisk clip.

"Well," Gail said from the van. "I guess that wraps it up. Let's go find some other diversion, Roger. Come."

But Casey walked up the dirt track to the fence, and stopped, no more than a foot from the foaming, awful jaws of those guard dogs. He kicked the chainlink with the sole of his shoe, which doubled their ferocity.

"Slick, give it a rest," Fenton called. "There's no way around these mothers."

"Poisoned meat," Casey said. "We could throw it over and kill 'em, then climb over and walk in."

"Who wants to," Kimball Johnson said. "I'm not going through all that to peep at some damned freak. The carnival will be through in the Fall."

"Yeah," Gail said. "If you can put a lock on your perverted desires until then." She laughed. "Besides, there are a couple of real women in this van, or haven't you noticed, little man?" She laughed again, her voice high and reedy from the weed and from fear. "You got the hots for Miss Spook or what?"

Casey targeted her with one of his stares. She shut up.

Fenton was getting bored. "Come on, man," he said. "Or walk home."

Roger Casey knew Fenton meant it, and he heaved a short sigh. But then he saw it. "Wait."

Something grey and large moved in the green of the pines. He felt the artery in in his neck pulse and the air pause in his lungs. Could they be so lucky?

She emerged from the treeline—but it was only another dog, its mane billowing: a big old dog, with something in its yellowed teeth. It wasn't immediately welcomed by the other dogs. Somebody else's dog maybe, or a wild stray.

"I'm not screwing around here, man," Fenton warned.

"Look—Jeeze, what a smelly hound."

"What's it got?" asked Gail, leaving the van to join Casey.

"A dress," he said, as the others came closer to see.

It was a plain white-cotton dress, undecorated except for some coppery red slashes across it. When the white dog merged with the others, they set about ripping the garment to shreds, as if to vent their rage at the unreachable intruders.

"What are those marks?" Alex mumbled. "They look like bloodstains."

"Could be," Casey said. "Maybe MaryAnn's blood."

"You think that's the freak's dress?" Kimball said.

"It's too small to fit the mother."

"Nobody ever sees her in anything but pants, anyway," Alex added.

Casey said, "MaryAnn hurt herself . . . or someone hurt her."

Fenton chuckled. "Maybe it's just her time."

Gail rolled her eyes. "All over her dress like that? That much? Sure."

"She's a freak, right?"

"Don't be disgusting, Fenton," Deirdre sighed.

"Okay," Fenton said, "let's roll," and they got back in the van and headed off, away from the direction Muriel Nelson had taken. A couple of miles along they came upon an abandoned car. It was off the road, partially obscured by branches.

"Camouflage," Casey announced, as they inspected it.

"What are you talkin' about?" said Kimball Johnson.

"They've been torn off the trees, thrown on the car deliberately so you wouldn't necessarily see it from the road." He stared up at the slope. No fence here, he thought.

"Nissan Maxima," Kimball said. "It's got rental tags. A cheapie, from Florida."

"But it's new looking," Deirdre said.

"Yeah," Kimball nodded. "This year's." He tried the doors. "Locked."

Deirdre gestured helplessly. "Why would anyone just abandon a new car?"

"Let's pop the trunk," Fenton said, and he and Alex proceeded to force it open, with some help from Kimball Johnson and the tire iron from the van. Deirdre grew more anxious by the second, as they strained against the lock.

"Dee," Gail said. "What's the matter with you?"

"What if there's somebody in it?"

The boys heard this but kept on. With a metallic groan, the lock gave way and the lid flew up.

"Oooo!" Deirdre jumped back; Gail, too.

Other than a screw-type jack and a miniature spare tire, there was nothing inside.

"Shit," Alex said and looked back at her. "*Don't* do that."

"KJ," Fenton said, "how about the hub caps, battery, whatever."

"Yeah," Kimball Johnson said. "I'll get the tools from the van."

But when they had opened the hood, they found that everything portable was gone, even the fan belts.

"Hey," Kimball said. "Where you going, Case?"

Roger Casey was slowly working his way up the heavily wooded hill.

"Follow the leader," Fenton said and started up after him. Only Kimball Johnson followed.

Single file, Casey in the lead, they followed what might have been an animal trail, or maybe a faint path. Trail, Casey decided, because it avoided the taller branches four-footed creatures wouldn't have worried about. Trail.

It led up, then made a distinct cut left—north—toward the Nelson place. After a quarter hour's hike, they came to a clearing filled with the tall stalks of winter corn. The crop had long ago been abandoned but the corn replenished itself. Uncultivated, it had overrun the field, growing thick and random, the neat organization obliterated. Here the trail became a distinct path, although it would have been invisible unless you had stepped onto it at the exact point they exited the woods.

Dwarfed by the stalks, the boys fell silent. The stillness inside the labyrinth of corn intimidated them. But Casey pressed on, and Fenton Lindsey followed almost gleefully, while Kimball Johnson stayed close out of pure fear: too terrified to turn back alone, to stop, to speak.

Maybe thirty paces into the field, Casey stopped and squatted down. Fenton and Kimball joined him, hunkering down alongside. Before them was an earthen circle cut from the growth, and packed hard. Atop the stalks ringing the perimeter were macabre clumps made of braided vines and weeds, and corn husks. They were unrecognizable at first: like bizarre dolls heads made of the plants and bones and bramble. Dangling from beneath many of these were the skulls of small animals, bleached white: possum, raccoon, badger, cat, squirrel, muskrat, skunk. At the top of the circle were two pits, equidistant from one another, maybe four feet deep. Nearer the boys was a third pit, larger than the other two, but the same depth, and black at the bottom like the others. Between the smaller two and the larger one stood a mound of stones, like a primitive grave perhaps, but rounder. Atop the mound were arranged the skulls of larger creatures: cows, horses, dogs, sheep, and the top of what might have been a small human cranium. Each bore odd designs in black.

"Motherfucker," Fenton whispered.

Casey stood to full height and walked about the circle, slowly observing, savoring. He realized now that the red earthen circle was oddly raised, like a pitcher's mound.

"Please," Kimball whispered. "Let's get out of here."

Fenton rose too, but stood in place, watching. Still squatting, Kimball clutched his shins with his hands and rocked on his heels, chin pressed against his knees. Casey completed his careful circuit and paused.

"What the hell is it?" Fenton said softly, both of them unable to look away from the circle.

"Holy ground," Casey whispered.

3

DEXTER SUTTON sat back on the couch in the office of his new district supervisor, Dr. Lola Aragon, and watched her quietly prep Mr. Porter Kolda, principal of Northview High. Sutton, chairman of the school board and a director of the state education commission, had wanted new blood in Duncan County, where he felt the local board had allowed a complacent mediocrity to impair the workings of the school system and the curriculum. He had wanted his new district supervisor to shake things up and she was certainly not unshy about it (confirming his judgement, he was pleased to note).

"Mr. Kolda . . ." she said from behind her desk, addressing the principal seated facing her, their ultimate boss casually draped on the couch as if he were hardly present. "Ah," she said, finding the reference in the file open on her blotter. "Here it is—MaryAnn Nelson."

"MaryAnn Nelson?" Kolda repeated slowly. "No, can't recall ever having heard the name. Why?"

"She lives somewhere in the western part of the county, in your district, and she's appeared on your annual list of exempted minors for the past decade. There wasn't an exact address on file. My secretary said the area where she lives is called 'the Thickets,' but that didn't sound terribly specific."

"No," Sutton volunteered from the couch, "it's a specific place. You know the area don't you, Porter? Over around Blue Tree Road and Cat's Peak. In that vicinity."

Kolda nodded uncertainly. "Yes. Yes, indeed," although he had never so much as driven in that direction in his life. "But I don't recall the name, nor do I know the family off hand. Duncan is a big county." He smiled politely; she didn't.

"I thought everybody knew everybody in the South," she said.

"Do you know everyone in Yonkers or Rockaway Beach?" Kolda replied, trying to sound friendly. "What's special about this MaryAnn Nelson?"

"Well, for one, she is apparently completely uneducated. Grade successfully completed: zero. Cumulative grade point average: zero point zero. And on 21 June she will be sixteen and thereafter beyond our influence, presumably to remain illiterate."

Porter Kolda racked his brain, trying to recall something — anything — about the name, but could only surmise that the child was the offspring of some impoverished family that had circumvented the school authorities and kept the girl out of the hands of the Philistines and in the fields of the Lord.

"Anyway," he said, "it would be rather late to make an effort now, wouldn't you say? Maybe her parents simply wanted her kept out of school.

"So it would appear." Lola Aragon took off her reading glasses. "But I'm not sure they are entitled to make such a decision. As you say, it's late in the game for MaryAnn Nelson, if she's educable. We are obligated to see if anything can be done for her, nonetheless. She should at least be taught to read, don't you think?"

Kolda shrugged philosophically. "It's nearing end of term. We're incredibly busy with—"

"I think," she said, "the matter should be looked into . . . soon."

Dexter Sutton removed his rimless glasses. "Let me get this straight. This kid is fifteen, nearly sixteen, and nobody even checked out why she never started school? When I was young, if I missed two days in a semester, there were people in my face demanding to know what was wrong."

"Your *parents,*" Kolda inserted deftly, keeping any possible blame at arm's length.

Lola Aragon held her glasses to her nose, and peered at the paper in her hand. "Her mother got some sort of medical exemption to keep her out of first grade and she's never bothered to enroll her child since."

"There's your problem," Kolda said, smugly. "She's retarded."

"That's not confirmed," Lola Aragon said. "And even if it were true, we can't just compromise her rights, as if she were nonexistent or useless. Mentally disadvantaged people have all sorts of opportunities today. It is an abrogation of our duty as educators to shunt them aside like shameful accidents.

Children aren't possessions. Parents can't dispose of them as they see fit."

"You're sounding a bit like the ACLU, Dr. Aragon," Kolda said, trying to smile. "This may be a case of simple economics: the child is needed to work the farm. Or the family has decided to protect its own from outside scrutiny.

Lola delayed responding, in an effort to center her emotions and suppress her reaction. "This girl has not attended school in sixteen years. She is not in a hospital. She is not dead. She is not being educated in some alternative way."

"Well," Dexter Sutton said in a folksy tone, "maybe she's 'mentally disadvantaged,' and maybe she's not. Either way, we've got to know." He gave them his best medium smile—as in, Work it out for yourselves. "What's next on the agenda for Northview?"

''NOT MUCH here," Claudette announced, walking in a file from the hall of records and depositing it on Lola's desk.

Lola Aragon put aside the notes she was making and undid the ribbon of the accordion folder.

"There's hardly anything, believe me," Claudette said, pointing with her chin at the paltry few items appearing from the folder.

"That's too bad." Her boss flipped through the scant pages.

"I've punched up everything I can from the data bank, and seen everybody I can think of who might have something on her. There is appallingly little information on the girl anywhere, aside from the birth data and the address, and one inconclusive fire department report of suspected arson out at the Nelson place about eight years ago. They are really out in the sticks. Out of sight, out of mind. But still there, according to the tax rolls. One solid bit—the man who signed the exemption when she was six, and also delivered her: Dr. Joseph P. Endicott, one of our most eminent southern gentlemen."

"That impressive?"

"Let me put it this way, if the Cabots had migrated to Georgia and changed their name, they'd be the Endicotts. Their bloodline is as old as their money."

"Does he still practice?"

"I don't know. Doubt it. The Endicotts aren't big on a whole lot of work. And he was always more interested in politics than medicine. He served a couple of terms as mayor, you know, and one as a state senator." A hint of suspicion entered her voice. "What have you got in mind, Dr. Aragon?"

"Just a short visit."

"He's not an easy man to see, or to talk to."

Lola smiled. "Watch my smoke."

Claudette made a face. "Why *are* you so interested? This youngster will be out our jurisdiction in a couple of months."

"Yep. That's exactly why."

A s h e drove the patrol car through the quiet and immaculately groomed roadway of the Pinedale Estate, Ross Walker had to admire Lola Aragon's nerve.

Arm resting on the open window, she said, "I appreciate this, Ross."

"No problem. It beats washing down patrol cars. After all, it's county business in a way."

They reached the driveway and Ross guided the brown and gold cruiser up to the call box by the gate. He depressed a red bar and was greeted by a welcoming voice. Ross cited their appointment with Dr. Endicott and the voice thanked him and instructed him to drive to the garage. The gates hummed open.

The drive to the house was long and led them through meticulously cared for lawns, trees bursting with buds and new spring growth. In another few weeks the landscape would be glorious. The house itself was a huge two-story affair of brown stone trimmed in white. A screened tennis court sat adjacent to the south wing, and next to it, a magnificently tiled sunbathing area, and a swimming pool bigger than the high school's. The heated water steamed in the chill spring air.

"Imposing," Ross Walker said. Lola Aragon didn't reply.

At the front entrance, they parked behind a gleaming black Mercedes. A man stood at the entry. He had a lanky slimness, sharp features, and snow-white hair.

"Yes," he said coolly in a deep voice.

"Dr. Endicott?" Ross said.

"No, officer. I am Matthews. The doctor is my employer."

"Oh, the butler," Ross said without thinking.

He nodded. "Whom shall I say is calling?"

"The Duke and Duchess of Windsor." Ross bared his teeth in a grin.

"I beg your pardon?"

"I'm Dr. Aragon of Duncan County Educational Services, and this is Deputy Sheriff "Duke" Walker."

"Yes, madame. The Doctor is expecting you. Please come in."

They followed the butler into the opulent foyer and into the south wing, and then into "the Westbury Den." After directing them to the far end of the palatial room, he asked them to be seated and left to inform his employer of their arrival.

Ross made himself comfortable on a chaise longue, his booted feet up on the chintz. "Look at this," he said, gesturing at the artifacts that surrounded them. "Some den. Looks more like an art museum." He touched an exquisite figurine of a prancing horse displayed on the low table alongside him. "I have a feeling, if I slipped and smashed this, I'd be signing over my paycheck to the good doctor for the next ten years."

"It's Tang, worth, oh, one or two million," she said, slapping his fingers away and brushing his boots off the chaise.

"Jesus," he said, getting up and backing away from the sculpture.

"These are incredible," Lola Aragon said quietly, eyes moving from object to object, painting to painting. "Homer, Bierstadt, Church, Frederic Remington, Sargent, Heade, Peale, Eakins . . . . Just superb."

"Expensive?" Ross said.

She smiled, half to herself. "Worth every penny."

Ross Walker roamed their corner of the vast room. "And there's the doc."

"Endicott?"

"Yep." He pointed to one of a series of ultra-realistic portraits of what appeared to be several generations of Endicotts painted by the same artist.

She walked over and examined the oil painting of their host. "Magnificent, too," she said, "but I don't recognize the artist." She took out her reading glasses and peered through without putting them on. "Here's the signature.... Can't read it, though. Wouldn't you know it. The painting is realistic in the extreme and the writing is as illegible as a prescription."

"Maybe Endicott did it himself," Ross suggested.

"Could be. He certainly knows his art. This is an extraordinary collection," she said, looking back out over the expanse of the room, every wall surface and table bursting with color and shape and genius.

"This is more my speed," Ross Walker announced. He was bent over, with his hands on his knees, next to a primitive sculpture standing on the parquet floor—a crude figure made of reddish clay. Its body and face were featureless, except for a surprised expression barely suggested by the simple depressions that served as eyes, and the zero of a mouth.

Lola Aragon stared intently at it, captivated by the stark power of the piece and its contrast to the rest of the works in the room. It was an exceptional sculpture, deceptively simple and deeply affecting, but totally different in spirit and style from the sophisticated pieces displayed throughout the room. Its presence among these other works said something about its owner. But what?

She glanced about. No Cycladic art, no pre-Minoan, pre-Columbian, Scythian, Celtic. Nothing ancient, and nothing truly modern. What was this sculpture doing here then? How odd.

Just behind the standing piece was a related work, she noticed, a bas relief positioned low on the wall, partially hidden by a wing chair. She stepped closer. The piece was made of the same clay, though slightly different in color. And the crowd of faces and bodies depicted were the same as the sculpture: round featureless faces, dark indentations for mouths and eyes, a crowd of mute supplicants staring hypnotically at the beholder. No irises, no eyeballs, but staring nonetheless—They were chilling. Silent and shrill. What did they want? She looked for a signature.

Footsteps approached. "Good morning, good morning. I am Joseph Endicott."

Ross Walker's good manners returned to him and he made the introductions. Wordlessly, Dr. Endicott, gestured them into a nearby sitting area.

"No," he said to her. "Do please sit here." He indicated the specific places he wished them to occupy. They were, Lola noted, seats facing the wall of Endicotts.

"Before we begin, may I offer you refreshments?"

"Nothing for me, thank you," Lola said. "Your collection has refreshed me already."

"How kind," he said, and looked to Ross.

"No thanks," Ross said.

Endicott grunted. "Well, then. You mentioned in our telephone conversation that you wanted information about Miss Muriel Nelson and her daughter. How may I be of help?" And he sat down in the wing chair, next to the primitive sculpture. They were now about the same height. He, in the darkest blue blazer and beautiful plaid shirt and solid, dark tie; the clay figure as if in muddy robes. He, layered with sophistication and charm; the figure, raw, naked.

"I need to know about MaryAnn Nelson. She is nearing 16, lives in the western part of the county still."

"Yes, of course," he said. "I could hardly forget her, or her mother."

Lola brightened. "We would be most appreciative of anything you might recall."

He nodded. "Yes, yes. Muriel Nelson came to this area, oh, about twenty years ago. She'd worked in the film industry, in Hollywood."

Ross squinted. "She was an actress?"

"No, no," Endicott replied. "She worked in animation and titles, that sort of thing, in order to support her first love." He paused, turning carefully to gaze up at the portraits of his ancestors and the one of himself. "She was a very fine artist."

Lola's gaze followed his gesture up to the portrait of Dr. Endicott.

"I sat for her, as did my parents and wife." He turned back to them. "Her realistic style, unfortunately, was not the vogue, at the time. She tried, but . . . . The art world is such a political quagmire. Muriel Nelson came to Georgia in order to gain a purchase on the New York art scene, somewhat naively through the back door, as it were. Perhaps she was less than candid with herself about attempting such a feat, given the odds." He shrugged, eyebrows raised. "She hoped to support herself as a portraitist. Invariably, the subjects would be prominent figures or, at the very least, from prominent families whose influence might open doors for her, or her pictures. My parents and I were among her first commissions. In fact, she had several more in this part of the state and she did quite well financially, but her career remained in limbo and she grew increasingly frustrated. Her failure to achieve the recognition and rewards she wanted was unwarranted, true. She was so very talented. But she seemed to take this out on herself in unproductive ways."

"Such as?" Lola said.

"Oh, after a while, refusing new assignments, offending people unnecessarily—the spiteful sorts of things unhappy individuals do to sabotage themselves. She did quite a good job of it, which of course only exacerbated her situation. From what I could gather, Muriel Nelson had always had problems relating to people. The difficulties . . . enlarged. She wrote vicious, accusatory letters to everyone she was acquainted with, and she would make irresponsible, distasteful calls at all times of the day or night until her telephone was eventually disconnected."

"They took away her phone for making abusive calls?" Ross said.

"No. For lack of payment."

"Was she paranoid?" Lola asked.

Dr. Endicott crossed his legs. "I'm not a psychiatrist; I can't say definitively. But she certainly had tendencies in that direction, yes."

Lola looked at the perfectly lit portrait of Dr. Endicott, twenty years younger. "What did she do then?"

Endicott sighed. "In truth, there was precious little work in Sturgis for someone determined to make a reputation on the level she coveted. Even Chattanooga, or any of the other nearby cities of some size, offered nothing. I advised her to look upon her stay here as a respite and to return to the major markets, if she was really serious about advancing in her career. She was approaching forty, feeling thwarted, and she was incredibly obstinate, I thought. It was also increasingly evident that she was pregnant."

"Hardly a crime," Lola said, more sharply then she'd intended.

Dr. Endicott smiled, somewhat patronizingly. "You are new to the South, Dr. Aragon. Despite the negative impressions occasionally projected by the media, I assure you no one condemned Miss Nelson. I will concede that there was still an onus attached to unwed pregnancy in those days, but she wasn't ostracized or injured by public reaction so much as she was hampered by her own fragile psyche." He made a helpless gesture. "Her relationships with others deteriorated even further. She stopped painting altogether."

"Hardly surprising," Lola observed. "Single, alone, carrying a child. Deserted by the father?"

Endicott nodded. "Yes. The father did not acknowledge her or the child." He looked genuinely pained, she thought. "Some of us tried to help," he went on. "My wife and I were tremendously admiring of her talent and we had developed a grudging fondness for her, even if her personality did not allow actual friendship. We pressed her to identify the father but she refused. Nor would she accept financial help from us and another couple, nor from any local church organizations. She called it charity."

"Poor woman," Ross said.

"It was tragic, really," Dr. Endicott said. "She had no other family, no one to turn to, nowhere to go. She'd had some capital, saved from her fees, and she had earlier acquired a large block of cheap land, purchasing it for the back taxes. It included a modest but comfortable house and a shed or barn she had used as studio."

"But she was alone," Lola said.

Endicott held his palms up in a helpless gesture. "It's what she insisted upon, Dr. Aragon. The further she got into her term, the more reclusive she became. She was offered free medical care by the county and refused even that."

"And there was nothing to be done, nothing to legally compel her to care for herself and her unborn child?"

"No," Endicott said, glancing away. "Nothing to my knowledge, although it shames me to admit, I did not pursue it as far as I should have. Or so I thought afterwards. Anyway . . . " His gaze returned to Lola Aragon. "I had heard nothing for several months, when I received an urgent telephone call."

"From Muriel Nelson?" Ross asked.

"Yes. I was hardly an obstetrician, but she knew no other doctors and wasn't finicky, to say the least."

"You delivered the baby at her home?" Lola said.

"In point of fact," said Dr. Endicott, "she delivered alone." Lola shook her head. "Amazing."

"She had even cut the cord and cleaned up the child before I got there. An extraordinary woman. But she wouldn't allow me to so much as take the poor creature to the hospital for observation."

"Poor creature?" Lola said, her head tilted inquiringly.

"I'm afraid so. Multiple teratological abnormalities. The defects were profound. It was remarkable that she'd even survived in utero. I never dreamed she would live to school age, much less reach adolescence." He glanced away, almost a look of reverie on his face. "I was actually startled when

Muriel Nelson contacted me the summer of the child's sixth birthday—about the education question. She had decided—and the board concurred—that MaryAnn would best be left outside the instructional mainstream."

"The child never attended school," Ross said.

"Correct."

Lola Aragon was non-plussed. "You mean she remained closeted. Hidden. As if she had been born into the fifteenth century."

"Muriel Nelson refused to consider institutionalization."

"There are schools, Dr. Endicott. Surely—"

"Dr. Aragon," Ross interrupted. "The doctor isn't to blame for the Nelsons's problems."

"True," Lola said, her face losing its look of fury. "I must apologize, Dr. Endicott."

He gave a dismissive wave. "Not necessary. You may even be right. One should never apologize for caring too much. I wish I had had some of the same passion sixteen years ago. MaryAnn might have been given the start in life she needed to cope with her disabilities. I was just too pessimistic about her prognosis."

"Because she survived birth?" Lola said. "Or because she is alive at all?"

He looked sad. "Because of counter indications later on."

"Such as?"

"Well, simply that, despite her cranial deformity, her skull might still have allowed for some development, some intellect. Again, my field is not psychology or the brain, but perhaps her savant tendencies were indicative of therapeutic possibilities. And now it's too late, really. Her physical development is nearly complete. She is nearly adult."

"What are you referring to?" Lola asked.

"There evidently have been some signs that, despite a mental capacity in the lowest range, Nature has compensated with amazingly overdeveloped powers in a narrow, surviving area."

"Like a savant?" she asked.

Ross squinched up his eyes. "An area like—?"

"Art," Endicott said, "art. I had occasion to attend a gallery opening in New York about five years ago. It was an exhibition of so called outsider art produced by severely impaired individuals."

"Mental patients," she said.

"Yes. Schizophrenic, hebephrenic, autistic—psychotics."

"Crazy people," Ross said. "Insane."

Endicott nodded. "Mostly. Yes."

"What does this have to do with MaryAnn Nelson?" she said. "I'm not following."

"Several of the pieces were hers. The gallery owner had represented her mother and had been prevailed upon to include them."

"Like that one?" Lola said, pointing to the standing figure—the primitive, clunky slab of hardened clay with the childish dabs for eyes and mouth, whose creator had somehow imbued it with primordial power and ethereal lightness, both to stunning affect.

Dr. Endicott's demeanor did not alter in the slightest. "Yes," he said. "I see you are quite intuitive, Dr. Aragon." And then he shifted in the wingbacked chair, and seemed somehow relieved, not emotionally but almost physically. He seemed lighter, less stooped by age.

"It may not be too late," Lola said very softly.

He smiled politely. "It would be nice to think that, but . . . if you could comprehend the extent of her problem. Perhaps a secluded life is the humane solution. God knows, an institutional alternative would hardly be that."

"I'm sorry," Lola Aragon said, "I can't accept that we can allow ourselves to be so . . . so primitive as to lock away the imperfect among us."

"Oh, come now. Isn't that what an institutional life would mean for her?" Endicott replied. "Being locked away? And isn't that her inevitable fate anyway, once her mother passes?"

"I don't know," Lola said. "You were her doctor. You decided. How?"

The room fell silent; a clock ticked somewhere far away. Dr. Endicott seemed to have concluded something. He rose from his chair and walked to an architect's desk that, Lola guessed, must have dated back to the American Revolution. He removed a business size envelope from a drawer and came back toward the sitting area.

He said, "I admire the dedication you've shown, Dr. Aragon. Honestly. And I am not trying to rationalize my own weakness or possible failing in this instance, but I would like you to know the truth about the child. You'll have to, if you're to persist in this. Her—what shall I call them?—difficulties, they are immense."

He held out the envelope. Lola Aragon was relieved to see that it was sealed. Still, she understood the responsibility, perhaps an impossible one, that was passing to her. Was this more than she had bargained for? She hadn't really thought this far ahead. A retarded girl hidden in the woods and denied her humanity, is what she had thought. Now she wasn't nearly so certain.

"You have to know," Endicott said, "if you're serious about pressing further."

She took the envelope. He paced back toward the wall of ineffably beautiful art, the small statue now like a sullen troll alongside his elegantly attired figure. When he turned, he was back-lit by the lights illuminating the paintings. The day had become overcast. The gold of his buttoned blazer shone and his eyes glistened.

"Those," he said, "are the photographs upon which the board based its decision."

"Doctor," she said, "there may be ways to help her. Do we have to look at these to decide if the poor girl deserves a chance at life?"

Dr. Endicott's polite smile was a faint line in the semi-darkness. "My dear," he said, "MaryAnn Nelson is a monster."

MAMA HADN'T come in once, not even to bring her some food. But then, she hurt so bad that she probably wouldn't have eaten anyway. Better that she lie beneath the sheets and hide her shame. Tiny fragments of light spilled through the uneven wallboards in places to guide her to the sink where she pumped some water and swallowed it to slake her thirst, then spilled some on her arms and shoulder to ease the pain of the welts. Not knowing how long it would be before she saw her mother again, she had used the pot as little as she could manage. Besides, it ached when she moved at all and when anything even lightly touched the swollen places.

Toward evening, the room got real black. No moon again. There were gas lanterns in the house but she didn't know anything about lighting them. Mama always did that, and Mama was gone. Wary of her bruises, she lay slowly back upon her bed and let the cooler night air soothe the pain in her flesh where the belt had bitten. She thought of the floorboards, slipping through to the dogs, and out their door, but she knew it would be some time before she dared. She thought she should be shamed by such a thought, even as she felt pleased at the realization that each season the time that elapsed, from one night outing until the next, was steadily growing shorter. She liked it more and more. What did this mean about her, she wondered. Was she getting badder?

The boys were barking. Was someone coming to taunt and throw rocks against the house again? It had happened long ago and only once, but each time now it came back to her whenever they barked in warning and she was locked inside. She thought to reach for the scythe she kept near her bed and remembered it wasn't there.

But the barks changed. The boys were relieved, MaryAnn, too. Mama was returning. She loved her mother, but she knew she herself had been mistaken to come into her Mama's life and to ruin it so. She pulled the sheet up over her nakedness and measured the pain the touch of it caused her, then pulled it tighter to make it hurt more.

Mama unlocked the door and came in with a gas lantern glowing brightly. MaryAnn sat up, holding part of the sheet over her head.

"Take that thing off your head."

MaryAnn complied. "I'm sorry, Mama," she whispered, apologizing for what her mother would see. The lamp was bright and stung her eyes, but she still could see the pain in Mama's face and how it turned to look elsewhere.

"Put this on," her mother ordered and tossed her something from a paper sack.

MaryAnn held it up with gleeful surprise. "A new dress. Mama! Thank you."

"You can't go naked. Only animals run naked."

MaryAnn pulled the dress on over her head.

"This, too."

A hood had appeared next to her pillow.

Her mother said, "I haven't had time to sew buttons on the dress, so be careful."

"Yes, ma'am," MaryAnn said, suddenly distracted by the scent of fresh groceries in the other room. Bananas, too. "I'm real hungry, Mama," she said in a quiet voice.

"Good." Her mother's voice sounded hard and strong, like she had to be to keep them both alive. "Maybe the pain in your belly will remind you how bad you've been."

"Yes, ma'am."

"Now sit—on the bed. I've got something else for you.

MaryAnn sat, anxious to see what else there might be for her. Her mother picked up something long from the burlap bag.

"Give me your foot."

77

MaryAnn extended her foot. Shoes! Could it be shoes? She hadn't had real shoes in a very long time.

"Your right foot, stupid. You know your right from your left, don't you?"

"Yes, ma'am."

Her mother took her firmly by the ankle with one hand and brought the chain toward it with the other.

"Mama."

She snapped a metal cuff around the ankle, and cinched it tight. It adjusted, like handcuffs.

"Mama, please. Mama. It hurts. Take it off. Please!"

The woman slapped her daughter's thigh, hard. "Shut up. Shut up or I'll get the belt. Do you understand me?"

"Yes, Mama." MaryAnn tried to keep her voice as steady and calm as she could.

"What do you expect me to do?" Her mother continued to mutter in a low and angry voice as she tethered the chain to the metal frame of the bed. "I can't put in a whole new floor. You'd just pry that up, too. Well, this will slow you down some." She pulled sharply at the chain to test it and the whole bed shook. "Just right."

"Mama."

"You've got enough slack to reach the pot and the sink, but I don't think you'll be crawling through any holes, unless you find one big enough to drag a bedstead through."

MaryAnn rubbed around the metal band biting into her flesh. "It hurts, Mama."

"Be quiet."

"But, Mama—"

"*Don't* you raise that hand! Not a finger. Lie down. Go to sleep."

"Please . . . Mama."

She didn't reply. Picking up the empty sack and the lantern, she left the room, locking the door behind her.

MaryAnn slowly worked the leg and chain beneath the bedsheets. Her lungs quivered, the metal hurt. What had she smelled, besides the bananas?

It wasn't other food. It was something else, something on Mama. Fear, she had smelled fear. Mama had been afraid.

HEARTBURN FROM a three chilidog and nachos lunch was inching up Jake Claypoole's esophagus with hot claws and spurs. He tried to work through it, as he had countless times during thirty years on the job. But this time it kept getting worse. Even noisy belches didn't relieve the heat or the pressure.

Think lovely thoughts, he told himself, as he sat on his ponderously idling bulldozer, and wondered at the amount of garbage that people could commit to the waiting earth over a single weekend, and how these mounds looked exactly like every other mound he'd buried in the last thirty years.

Five more years to go, just five until he hit sixty. He'd have put in twelve thousand, seven hundred, eighty-three work days, all told.

The pain hadn't lessened, just climbed higher. Damn. It was beginning to affect his work and tease him with possible causes: heart attack? flu?

While leveling another of the self-propagating mounds of refuse, he was so gripped that he made a mistake that might have caused even a new operator acute embarrassment.

Working in the area he had already covered that morning, he eased out too far onto soft ground. The machine tilted forward, like a submarine about to dive.

"Whoa."

Jake hurled every epithet at the beast, as he slammed into reverse. For an instant the caterpillar treads fought for a grip in the red earth, and he pictured what it would be like to flip, ass over elbow, into the reeking garbage. Instinctively, he levered the huge front blade downward like a hammer, trying to strike through the goop into the hard soil beneath, and force the dozer's tail back down.

He was about to abandon ship, and take his chances outside the cage, when the treads caught and the great machine lurched back onto a solid footing, the blade ripping a trench through the covered garbage with its uppercut. Smelly dirt and dust flew everywhere.

Jake sat in the idling machine, trying to regain his composure. Colleagues had leapt off their own dozers and were racing across the landfill toward him.

"You okay?" Frank Wanderei shouted. "Jeeze, that was close. You all right?"

"Yeah, yeah," Jake grunted and cut the motor. The heartburn now felt like he'd swallowed a blowtorch. The hell with this silent suffering, he decided, and swung off his seat, dropping to the ground on shockingly weak legs.

The other guys knew it was not the time to stand around, compounding an old pro's embarrassment. So they laughed it off and turned back to their own work. Jake leaned on the huge tread for support, wondering if he was dying, and decided to get his butt over to the operations shack and call a doctor. Testing his watery legs, he stepped away from the machine, onto something dredged up by the blade. It felt funny, even beneath his workboot.

It was a hand. Complete, from the wrist on, the fingers long and slender. The bits of red nail polish seemed to glow against the flat white of the hand itself.

Continuing on, past the front of the blade, he looked down into the pit that his near-accident had excavated, and vomited everything in his stomach right into it.

THERE WERE already two other teams of deputies and some city police on the scene when Deputy James Lowell drove through the gates of the dump. He parked a good thirty yards away from the site and walked carefully across the baked red clay to reach the yellow bulldozer and the gash it had torn into the piles of rubble and the earth beneath. Around it had gathered all the onlookers and lawmen. The sight of what lay at the bottom was only exceeded by the ripe smell that hung over the landfill.

"God," Lowell said, screwing up his face.

"Yeah," Les Blankenship agreed.

There were two human trunks in the slit, partially covered with clay and garbage and somebody's idea of lunch. One torso was slight and female, judging from the single breast remaining intact. The second was considerably larger, but so desperately mutilated and lacking genitalia that it was impossible to surmise its gender with certainty. Just then one of the boys was unlucky enough to unearth the head, stuck in the ungodly muck between the female torso and a crushed toilet seat cover.

The head was mercifully draped in part with its own long, reddish-brown hair and beard, but it was pretty evident the lips, nose and eyes were gone.

"Talk to me, Les," said Jim Lowell.

"That pasty-faced fella talking to the city boys over there, he turned them up less than an hour ago. He figures they were left here sometime over the weekend, buried under one of the first piles of garbage that he covered. It was only dumb luck that he dug them back up. There's probably a lot of assorted pieces still buried under here."

"No clothes?"

Les Blankenship shook his head. "No sign of them yet. I doubt that we'll find any."

"Were they already cut up this way, or did he do it with his blade?"

"The coroner will tell us, but my guess is that they were in pieces when they arrived."

"I know this is a stupid question, Les, but you got any idea as to the cause of death?"

Blankenship grinned, a funereal smile. "That's a stupid question all right."

"Who's caught it?"

"Baker and Dantzler got here first, but some of the city guys are claiming it for themselves, because of the rezoning session last month. We'll have to wait and see how the cards fall, I guess."

"They . . . shit, they look eaten," Lowell said. "What's been at them?"

Blankenship tugged down the brim of his Smokey the Bear hat. "Hell if I know. Maybe rats, or the stray dogs that scavenge here at night."

4

" I ALWAYS wanted to be a teacher," Lola said, over dessert at the quiet restaurant Ross had selected. No band, no piped in music, just quiet.

"Any particular kind?" he said, sawing at his peach pie.

"The involved kind. After college I joined the Peace Corps."

"You're kidding. Nobody joins the Peace Corps anymore."

She laughed. "I did. They sent me to Uruguay. I helped to dig a well and tried to teach the basics to a few kids who possessed a lot more in the way of survival skills than I did. After my hitch, I came home and did a little more classroom work and toiled at more degrees. The administrative area grew more attractive. God knows, it paid better. Then I met a debonair art dealer named Eddie."

Ross made a point of stuffing his mouth.

"Thanks," she said.

"For what?"

"Not asking. But I might as well tell. Unless I'm boring you, Deputy."

"Not at all, Doctor. I've yet to discover anything about you that is boring."

"What a gent. Anyway, Edward Fields is every girl's dream. Six-one, sculpted. Very social, successful. We meet at a party. He likes my opinions about his clients' work and six months later we're husband and wife. Everything was fine . . . ." She glanced down. "Maybe not so fine—we had a lot of fights, even the first year. Checking account, laundry, that sort of stuff, but the animosity was out of proportion to the issues. Year two, I find out we're pregnant."

"How did Eddie take it?"

"He said the right things, went through the motions, but he wasn't head over heels in love with idea. I didn't like seeing that, so I refused to see it for a while, but . . . . There were complications with the pregnancy. A chromosome test revealed problems. Eddie instantly pushed for an abortion, which was certainly the sensible thing, the wise decision—all that. Except it's a little more primal than that for a woman. We fought some more, but really seriously now. He was not about to accept a lifelong burden simply to indulge my sentimentality. Especially since he was so perfect, such a physical specimen. The doctors gave their considered opinions, the counselor we saw had her say, and Eddie ranted every day—before work, after work, on the way home from openings." She shook her head. "He was right. And he was an insensitive shit."

"That's a tough situation," Ross said, his chin resting on his hand. He fussed with the ashtray.

"So I went to church to make my peace. Then I did it. Edward was happy. I left him the day I got out of the hospital."

Ross hid behind his uplifted coffee cup, downed the last of it, and set it back on the saucer. "So you decided to try southern climes."

She brushed back her hair from her eyes. "I had an approach from Dexter Sutton via a recruiter. He wanted someone to challenge the status quo. My forte. I thought the pace down here would suit me."

"I hope we haven't been too challenging so far," Ross said, smiling.

"Hey, I didn't say I wanted to spend my life in a coma."

He chuckled. She waited a moment and decided to chance it. "So," she said, leaning forward on her elbows. "What's your story, Deputy Walker?"

"Hey, Boss!" a voice interrupted: James Lowell. The deputy was sauntering over, his arm around the waist of his wife, Patricia. "How's it coming?" he said.

Ross and Lola grinned back at him. Ross said, "Slow. How about you?"

"A-number-one, fella. Listen, you two got any plans for the immediate future?"

"I'm Patricia," said his wife.

"Oh." Ross rose abruptly. "I'm sorry. This is Lola Aragon. Lola—Patricia Lowell."

"Hi," Lola smiled.

Patricia sat down in the chair her husband slid over from an empty table. He plopped into one himself and said, "We're thinking of goin' over to Jeremy's Place." He looked from Lola to Ross with a hopeful expression. "How about you, me, Lola and Patti going out for a little hell-raising?"

"I'm kinda bushed," Ross said.

"Is this Ross Walker talking?" James Lowell arched his eyebrows in mock surprise.

"Excuse me," Lola said, rising.

"Are you gonna powder your nose?" Patricia said.

"Actually, I was thinking of peeing."

Patricia laughed aloud. "I'm with ya."

The women left. Lowell eyed them. "Hoo-eee, that is some fine stuff strutting there," he said. "Just look at that, Ross."

"I'm looking, buddy." Lola Aragon, walking away, *was* an impressive sight.

"Man, with those Mexican looks and that fine form, I could get real close to that. You'd better believe it."

"I don't know," Ross said. "It seems to me she's interested more in us intellectual types."

"More power to you, buddy. Now, how about Jeremy's. We could do some dancing and maybe catch some glimpses of new behinds. We're getting behind in our behinds, you know."

"James, I think you've got this hangup." Ross said.

"And I think you're caving in to middle age already. What are you—pushing thirty-one?"

"I hit thirty-two last February."

Lowell made a face. "That's painful to think about. I think we'd better not waste any opportunities, like tonight."

The women returned and it was quickly decided they would give Jeremy's a try. Lola supposed it would be a redneck roadhouse, but Jeremy's turned out to be a large, sunken room with subdued light, at least fifty round tables, soft background music and an elegant hostess receiving them by the door. The place was actually calm as they crossed to their table. No drunken brawls, no caterwauling singers. From the adjoining room the sounds of more aggressive merrymaking did filter through the swinging doors: the dance hall half of Jeremy's. But even this music seemed closer to rock than twangy country.

Patricia and James hadn't eaten yet, so they ordered dinner; Ross and Lowell kept them company, nursing cognacs.

"Aragon is Hispanic, isn't it?" Patricia asked.

Lola nodded. "That's right. It's Mexican. My father and his family came to New York from Matamoros when he was seven."

"Is your mom from there, too?"

"Oh, no. Mom is second generation Italian. Well, Sicilian actually."

"You know," James Lowell said, "I'm not even sure where my family originated.

His wife chortled. "Probably somewhere where food was plentiful and cheap."

Her husband grimaced. "Very funny. Like I was saying, I know very few people who can trace their family trees back more than a generation or three. But people who live up North can tell you where their granddad's great granddad lived."

"It wasn't always that way," Patricia said. "Bloodlines were really important to families before the War."

Lola looked quizzical. "The Civil War?"

"No!" Patricia laughed. "World War Two."

After Patricia and Lowell had finished, they all moved into the dance hall. The house band was five pieces, all acoustical, and not a banjo or fiddle among them. After three numbers, they were sweaty and exhausted from dancing. Ross motioned them to a table, where they happily collapsed.

A short man with battered features appeared, his face and balding skull etched with white scars. He was Jeremy Carrigan, the owner, a retired light-heavyweight boxer with over a hundred professional bouts. Despite his forebidding looks, he was a very nice man. "Y'all havin' a good time?" he said, and everyone assured him they were.

"What a nice host," Lola said and Jeremy Carrigan bowed.

Ross said, "Old Jeremy is a respected businessman, the soul of propriety, mostly. But a couple of times a year some young loudmouth will challenge him just a little too hard to ignore, and Jeremy will take a drink, then a lot of drinks, then beat up the idiot, and me and some of the other guys have to arrest him."

"Oh, dear," she said.

James Lowell shrugged. "It does help break up the monotony."

Jeremy Carrigan slapped him on the shoulder and spoke to Lola Aragon. "I've been getting challenges since the first time I stepped in a ring. Fighters scare people. Yeah, even an old, dried up piece of beef jerky like me. And scared people are hostile. They figure if they can bluff me down, it adds to their stature. They think I'm past it, just because I'm sixty-two."

"So what do you do?" Lola asked.

"Try to let it slide." He glanced toward the bar. "Like that leadhead there."

They all looked over, too — at a raw-boned farm boy staring

back at Jeremy Carrigan. "Gimme another banger," the youth loudly commanded the bartender, eyes fixed on Carrigan.

"Man, I'd like to," Carrigan said in a voice only those at the table could hear. "I don't know him from Adam's housecat, but you learn to smell these things coming. That boy's soaked up enough alcohol and prodding from his buddies to prove his manhood by taking on the old pug."

The bartender was motioning widely as he refused the farm boy's business, offering him coffee or Coca Cola instead. The hulk was having none of it.

"Ah oh," Patricia said. As if on cue, the farmer started toward Jeremy.

A waiter brought more drinks. As he set them out, he said to his boss, "He's back again, Mr. Carrigan."

"You know," Ross said, "with all the trouble these sots cause you, why don't you just give up your liquor license?"

Jeremy looked aghast. "And have everybody find out that my cooks can't toast bread. No way. I'll put up with the odd drunk to keep out of the workhouse."

"Want me to take care of him?" Lowell asked.

"Don't bother, son. Some things just have to happen, sooner or later. Don't worry. I'll shine him on. I never break up my own place."

Then the ruddy-faced, crew-cut tough was upon them.

"You the owner?" he demanded, in a voice like half congealed molasses.

"That's me, Jeremy Carrigan." He extended his right hand. Sometimes that was enough. "Who might you be?"

The hand was not accepted.

"I might be Hayden 'The Hawk' Kondracke, and I want to find out why some withered piece of horseleather like you is supposed to be the toughest two-legged bastard around."

"Me?" Carrigan asked in feigned shock. "Friend, I haven't been tough since Fiona Elizabeth Boyette threw a net around me thirty-six years ago. Now she whips my ass good every night."

"Every night?" Ross said.

Carrigan raised an eyebrow. "Well, three times a week, anyway."

Young Hayden 'The Hawk' Kondracke was confused. "Let's don't mess around with this thing, old man. I got people riding my ass because of you, and we both know there's only one way out of it. Or are you sayin' you're not the guy who used to be a fighter?"

Carrigan smiled. "Back in my misspent youth I used my head for a punching bag. But I had brain cells to spare then."

Kondracke decided all this was somehow at his expense; he was angry. "Man, I've cleaned the clocks of cops, football players, honkeys, niggers and chinks, but I never beat up on a for-real boxer. Especially one who's cut off my liquor."

Carrigan draped an arm across the young man's shoulders. The homeboy was a couple of inches taller, maybe six-four, and he weighed in the area of two-thirty. It didn't look like anything close to an even match.

The older man leaned in to Hayden Kondracke in fatherly fashion. "Listen, shithead. I'd like to get you so blind drunk that you'd miss the floor when you fell, but it ain't gonna happen tonight. Now, if you want to vomit up that garbage and keep drinking, you take it out in the alley where it belongs. And if you really want some of me, you come back when you can piss without drowning both feet. Try me now and I'll feed you every last tooth you got. You hear me?"

Lola cheered, startling everyone.

Hayden Kondracke colored. "You want it here, or out where we won't bust up the furniture and stuff?"

Carrigan grinned. "Think it'll go that long?"

"I don't think you'll last long enough to hiccup, grandpa."

Two other toughs stepped toward them from the bar. Not a good sign, Lowell thought, and slipped out of his chair to block the way. Ross was suddenly not there either, Lola realized.

"You're standing in my way, lardass," said the taller one to James Lowell. They were about as close as they could get without kissing.

"Yeah," said the other one, blocked by Ross, "get the load out of the way or apply for a zip code."

The two young men laughed at their own wit.

"Just take it easy, fellas," Ross said. "Nobody's looking for major trouble."

"Who asked you, butthole?" Kondracke sneered, pressed against Carrigan, over whom he towered.

Ross let his jacket drift open, exposing the shoulder holster he was required to carry at all times.

"Oh," the youth facing him said, a sudden innocent look on his face.

"That's Deputy Butthole to you," Ross said.

"Sure," said the young man, instantly agreeable.

Not catching what had transpired, Kondracke was livid. "Goddamn!"

"Shut up," whispered his friend. "Forget it, Hayden. Walk away." They tugged on his arm.

Taking the hint, Kondracke said, "Yeah. Okay. Old man, some other time."

"Just a minute," Ross said as they started away. They looked at him. "You owe this gent and these ladies an apology.

Jeremy shook his head. "No need."

"I'm waiting," Ross said.

The three seemed ready to detonate. But the short one, the most level-headed, muttered, "We're sorry, all of us. It was a stupid way to act." He glowered at Ross. "Enough?"

Ross nodded, and the trio retreated to the bar.

"Well," James Lowell said, "where were we before all the fun started?"

"We were going home," Lola said, looking only at Ross Walker.

The party broke up and they went their separate ways, Ross and Lola in the direction of his place. The neighborhood was nice. They parked out front and climbed the external flight of stairs to the second floor. The apartment was sparsely furnished except for an expensive double-loading video cassette machine and an extensive library of movie tapes.

"Early bachelor," Lola said, taking in the collection. "Some of it bootlegged, I see." She touched the box marked with a handwritten title. "Anything salacious?" she said, arching her eyebrows.

"No ma'am," he called out over the noise of the coffee maker. "Say, you look at those photos yet—of the kid?"

"No," she said. "Why do you ask?"

"No reason. Just curious."

"I'm thinking about it."

He brought out the tray of cups and the pot. She settled herself on the couch and he knelt by the low table to pour. Although the mutual attraction was obvious, they were nervous. Over coffee they even ran out of small talk and lapsed into an uneasy silence. They hadn't so much as kissed.

Finally he cleared his throat and said, "Lola . . . are you sure? I mean, I'm not exactly . . . . I don't think . . . ."

Dr. Lola Aragon said nothing. She got up and turned off the living room light, then pulled her blouse out of the waistband and undid the buttons.

''THE NELSON girl?" the gas station man said, "She's a killer."

"You've seen her, Mr. Wiley?" Roger Casey said. "Or is this a story?"

"No story," the man said, slightly hunched over the hose fitted to the van's gas tank intake. The numbers sped by on the pump next to them. The kids in the van peered out of the windows, listening to the hick Casey had engaged in conversation.

"Yep," the man said after a while. "It was 'bout a year ago. A Wednesday night. I was driving down from Tennessee. On the county road, near the Thickets, something solid white jumped out of the dark and landed on the road right in front of me, right into my headlights. Wow. It was so sudden and bright. Like a flashbulb popping right in my eyes, you know?"

"Yeah," Casey said.

"She turned to look straight at me. I slammed on the brakes and the horn at the same time. The car went into a skid." He extracted the nozzle and set it back in its cradle on the pump. "It wasn't human." He shook his head. "The thing I saw wasn't human . . . not really."

"Was she wearing her hood?"

Mr. Wiley gave a small, sad smile. "Wish she was." His expression darkened. "There was fresh blood all over her mouth and throat. And she was holding something dead . . . 'bout the size of a kid.

"Dear God," Deirdre whispered, but loudly enough for everyone to hear.

"I . . . when I got the car swung back around, she was gone. The woods were black as sin. So I hot-rodded home, knowing I had to call the troopers or the sheriff. But by the time I got there, I'd convinced myself my eyes had been playing tricks, that she'd really been holding a rabbit or a dog or something."

"Yeah," Casey said, paying out the total run up on the pump. "Much obliged." He got back into the front passenger's seat and Fenton Lindsey pulled away before the door was even shut.

"Jeez," Gail said.

"What do you think, Case?" Alex said.

Casey shrugged. "The guy was undoubtedly running white lightning. Sampling his own hootch maybe."

"And maybe not," Kimball Johnson added. "Hell, bad moonshine can make you blind but it don't make you nuts."

Alex looked at his watch. Three forty-eight on a Monday. Monday always was a shitty type of day. Most of the students at Northview High School came in on Monday mornings still half-wasted from the weekend's recreation, but the damned teachers always showed up with the attitude that it was just another day to pack with droning lectures, rote recitations, tests, phys ed, yes-sir no-sir crap and related trivia. By the afternoon you needed another weekend just to get ready for Tuesday. So when they'd piled into Fenton's van at a little past three, the gang knew Fenton Lindsey's gas would be carrying them some place that, in all likelihood, Roger Casey would have decided on. Because Fen was the leader but he wasn't the brains. It was his van, his money, his family reputation that got them into places and out of jams, but the ideas for their outings came from the most off-center dude among them. Roger Casey, the idea man. "The Head" was a few bricks shy of a load.

"Alex, my man" Fenton said to him. "Give me a hit of something quick, before my memory clears and I realize that you owe me a yard.

Alex Schneider looked greatly apologetic. "Sorry, Mister L. I'm running on empty myself."

Fenton looked away, as if resigned to sobriety and then whipped about quickly to rap Alex's head with his knuckles.

"Listen, jerkoff," he said quietly. "You're not here to give me lame excuses. You contribute to the party or find somewhere else to sponge, right?"

"Okay, okay," Alex mumbled. "Don't worry. I'll find something."

"Leave him alone," Deirdre interjected. "It won't do you any harm to spend one afternoon in the land of the living."

"Where are we going?" said Gail Parker. Fenton floored the accelerator.

"Vroom, vroom," Kimball Johnson hooted. "Damn, let's go to Gongtown."

Deirdre made a face. "God, I hate that place. Besides, they're still pissed at you, KJ, for that fight last time."

"Hey. No arrest, no conviction."

Alex Schneider, still smarting from the reprimand, was eager for one of Casey's classic weird runs to get Fenton's mind off them.

"Gongtown," Kimball yelled.

"No," Casey said. "Keep going on this."

"What fuckin' loony tune picnic are we goin' on now?" Kimball said.

"Tell, me Kimball," said Casey, sounding contemptuous. "What do you stuff your jock with?"

Disbelief flashed on Kimball Johnson's face. His big hands were suddenly fists and he slammed them against the back of Roger Casey's seat. "You don't talk to me like that. I'll smash you, man. I'll do it."

Kimball Johnson was a big eighteen year old, Roger Casey was half his size and a head shorter, yet he seemed unaffected by the other's threat. Casey just gazed evenly at the red-faced teenager being restrained by Gail and Alex.

"Cut it out," Fenton ordered. "Stop busting up my van."

"Yeah," Kimball sneered. "Sure. But you remember, you little ass bite. I'm not taking your shit."

Casey, half turned in his seat, grinned. Using his hand to mime a gun, he aimed at Kimball and softly said, "Bang."

"I'm gonna pop him!" Kimball Johnson bellowed. "I mean it."

But of course he didn't. No one ever knew what Roger Casey might do next, or to whom, and nobody wanted to find out.

"Cool off, man," Fenton said. Then, to Casey, "How much longer?"

"The next bend."

They were somewhere in wooded hills. "Here?" Kimball demanded angrily. "We drive for damn near two hours to get here? What are we gonna do, get romantically involved with a bunch of farm animals?"

"That would beat your usual date," Gail said, and they all laughed, including KJ.

A half mile later Casey told Fenton to stop at a small farmhouse that came into view. Alongside it was a fenced pasture. There were cows grazing, and a number of distrustful chickens in a wire pen on the opposite side of the house. There were no vehicles in the yard or the open barn. No one around.

"What's the deal?" Fenton said, obviously less than satisfied with the once inventive Roger Casey. What Fenton Lindsey had no use for, he discarded, and Casey was rapidly approaching the line.

"Yeah," Kimball joined in, "why'd we waste a whole afternoon driving to this outdoor rectum?"

Casey open his door and pulled his shoulder bag into his lap. "You'd better get some mud on the license plate," he said to Fenton, then slipped out. The others scrambled out after him.

"So we won't be identified doing what?" Alex called. "What's going to happen, man?"

Roger Casey walked to the fenced in pasture, the others straggling after. The cows looked at him, but the new arrival wasn't impressive enough to hold their dull-witted attention for long. They returned to grazing.

Casey set the bag on the ground, pulled a pair of black leather gloves from his pocket and zipped open the flap. From the shoulder bag he removed a handgun.

"Wow," Alex marveled. "It's real."

Fenton and Kimball Johnson, who had handled guns most of their lives, turned bored looks on Alex Schneider. Fenton leaned on a fence post.

"What are we shooting, man?"

Casey held the weapon in its two main parts. "This, dearly beloved, is a Colt government model Mark IV, Series 70, semi-automatic, recoil-operated, locked breech, single-action, exposed-hammer, air-cooled handgun." Kimball applauded insolently. "It's especially adapted for this silencer, takes a seven shot straight-line box clip. Here's the thumb safety." He showed them the feature on the side of the gun. "It's a thirty-eight caliber with plenty of knock-down power."

"That's great," Alex said, admiringly.

Fenton exhaled. "I'll try it again. What are you shooting, Slick?"

Roger Casey screwed the silencer into place. He checked the magazine, faced the pasture, raised the gun and fired at a cow no more than five feet from him.

There was an airy zip, not very unlike the silenced firings they'd all heard on TV and in the movies. Then a wet bursting noise created by the bullet tearing through the cow's left eye and into its brain, followed by the dead thud of the animal's body dropping to the ground.

The other four cows seemed not to notice, and moved in a dimly curious fashion toward their fallen companion.

"All right!" said Gail, exhilarated, and rushed to the fence.

"Son of a bitch," Kimball Johnson muttered. "Ain't you a cold dude."

Casey aimed the gun and fired again. The bullet glanced off the second cow's heavy skull, sending it to its knees, stunned. The other cattle did take notice of this and did a leaden-hooved dance backward. Casey fired again, but missed completely.

Fenton chuckled and took the pistol from him without a word. He sighted quickly and killed the stunned cow with a bullet in the brain that sent the three others bounding into the pasture.

"Let me shoot it, too," Gail said eagerly.

"Everybody will get a turn," Alex said. He was looking into the open shoulder bag. "There must be a dozen clips in here."

"This is sick," Deirdre exclaimed, and returned to the van.

Fenton squeezed off a round at one of the fleeing cows and brought it down with a shell in its flank. It lowed weirdly.

In the forty-five minutes Casey told them they had, before the proprietors returned from town, they stalked and killed the two surviving cows, destroyed a dog, and picked off the chickens one by one as they ran and squawked hysterically within their wire enclosure. Everyone got several turns, except for Deirdre, who watched it all from the van, and Roger Casey, who watched only their faces.

MURIEL NELSON sat the bowl of broth on the table while she worked the lock to MaryAnn's door. It was awfully quiet in there, had been for over a day. No sounds of turning in bed, pumping water into the sink, or the jingling of the chain as she moved about.

Muriel pushed open the door, dropped the key back into her pocket and took the bowl in her free hand. Inside, the lantern cast its strong, yellowish light across the fierce giant forms drawn in charcoal on the walls: skulls, spinal columns, claws. The smell from the unemptied pot was pungent. The girl was on the bed, her figure small, hidden by the sheets, still.

She didn't move at all. Muriel could not detect the rise and fall of her breathing. Maybe it had been too much this time, she thought—the beating and the lack of food. Maybe the joke was over. She went closer and set the lantern behind the sink, at the head of the bed. Gently, she pulled the sheets off her daughter. The girl moaned softly within her dream. She was alive; it went on.

Carefully, Muriel drew aside the sheets. She was shocked to see the change. The skin was milk white, the bruises purple from the punishment. Her arms and legs looked as thin as branches of a small tree. The cuff that had been so tightly cinched now looked loose.

"Wake up," she said.

The girl tried. Her eyes, enormous and hollow within the hood, trembled. She made sounds. Heaving a long sigh, Muriel folded back the front of the hood until the mouth was exposed. Even now, after all these years, Muriel had to pause and collect herself. With one hand, she raised her daughter's head from the pillow and spooned a little broth to her lips. MaryAnn licked the warm liquid and parted her lips for more. Muriel fed her as if she were a baby.

A baby.

Muriel spooned the child nourishment and wondered where dead dreams went. Yes, this was her child, now sucking at her food with the uncoordinated urgency of an infant lapping. But this had never been remotely connected to a dream, and it was almost over. Muriel knew it in her bones.

MaryAnn's hands moved to the bowl, as if to pull it to her lips, but Muriel had no difficulty brushing them aside.

"Mama?" the girl sighed. Her eyes struggled to focus.

"I'm here."

"I thought . . . . I thought you'd left me." She sighed. "Don't ever. Never leave me, Mama."

"Everything's okay. I'm with you."

"I know," MaryAnn said, and accepted more broth. She ate in silence for a long while, every spoonful increasing her strength. She moved her legs slowly; the chain clinked. "Can I take it off, Mama?"

Muriel Nelson examined her daughter's lower leg. The skin was a white as the bellyflesh of some cave-dwelling creature, everywhere but the lines the belt had made and where the cuff had chafed and it was red and raw, with points of blood spilling onto the bedsheets. The scabs were half-formed, worn away by continual contact with the cuff, but there was no streaking, indicating infection, no blood poisoning. Not yet.

"Am I gonna die, Mama?" MaryAnn asked, so solemnly and matter-of-fact that Muriel almost laughed.

Die? MaryAnn had never really seen a doctor in her life. She'd never been immunized. She had recovered from fevers, viruses, illnesses and even, Muriel suspected, broken bones.

She healed quickly and seemed to mend so fast that Muriel had sometimes wondered if she *could* be permanently injured.

"I won't cry," the girl whispered, "if I am dying. I promise."

"Damn," Muriel said. "You're healthy as a horse. You won't need to worry about dying for a long time, and not at all while I'm alive."

Behind the hood, MaryAnn's face was unknowable.

"But you remember what they're going to do to you after I'm gone, don't you?"

"I remember."

Muriel looked closely at the angry flesh around the ankle. "We'll need to get something on this, some medicine and a bandage."

"Can I take off the chain? Please?"

"Not yet. You have to learn your lesson."

"I'm sorry."

"Maybe in a few days. After you've been punished and you've earned my trust again."

"I'll try."

The broth was about half gone. Muriel placed the spoon in the bowl and set it aside.

"I'm still hungry, Mama."

"You don't need anymore just now. It could make you sick." The woman stood from the bed. "I'll slop out your pot this one time."

"Mama?" The voice was still weak. MaryAnn struggled to sit up. "Can I have my tools?"

Muriel considered for a moment. Normally, depriving the girl of her chalky stones and charcoal, and the odd sculpting implements she had collected and forged over the years, was a part of punishments. But this disciplining had lasted longer than most. The girl was older, stronger; she could endure more, and it took more to restrain her. One day she would turn. Not letting her have her skinning knife and cutting wires and the other paraphernalia she used for her play-art was pointless. She would contrive substitutes if they were withheld and secret them away. There was nothing she couldn't hide when she wanted it to disappear, including herself.

"I'll bring you a few in the morning," Muriel said. She touched the cuff around the ankle and could feel the hope and excitement rushing through her daughter's body like an incoming wave. "We'll take this off now," Muriel said.

MaryAnn held her voice level. "Thank you, Mama. I think that would be good. I really did learn a strong lesson."

"Maybe we'll move it to the other leg, or one of your wrists."

The hope drained away. "Oh. Do we . . . do we have to? I mean, I know how you want me to be good. And it really hurts."

"I suppose you'd promise to behave," Muriel said skeptically.

"Oh, yes, ma'am. Promise. I will never go outside in the light. Only at night. And I will not let anyone harm us."

"Can I trust you? What about when I have to be gone. When I have to go to town for our food, or to forage for wood and batteries, and gasoline for the generator?"

"Even then. 'Specially then. I will guard the house—always."

"So I can trust you again?"

MaryAnn nodded.

Muriel stared hard at the girl in the stark light of the gas lantern. "I can see through you, you know. I can look straight into that brain of yours and hear what you're thinking."

MaryAnn said nothing, tried to think nothing.

"You've been very bad."

MaryAnn sat silent.

"If you defy me once more, I'll punish you again, with the belt and *four* of these." Muriel clanked the chain. "You might stay in this bed forever."

MaryAnn gazed past her at the open door of her room and the front door beyond.

"If you did that again, defied me again, I would leave you and never come back. Never." She paused. "Then it would all happen to you, everything I've told you."

The girl's voice was tired: "I'm sorry I was terrible. I won't do terrible things anymore, ever."

Muriel laid the chain at the foot of the bed. "All right, we'll test you."

MaryAnn's eyes leaped to her mother's face. "Really, Mama? No more of it for now?"

"For now," Muriel said. "But we'll have this here, just to remind you."

"Yes. I promise." She reached out as if to touch her mother, but Muriel eased out of her reach.

"I'll get something for your leg."

"Thank you, Mama. Mama . . . ?"

"What, MaryAnn?"

The girl touched the front of her hood, still folded up away from her mouth. "Would you brush my hair?" the lips said, the interior tissues of the mouth visible.

The refusal was on her tongue when Muriel stared into the eyes peering out of the slits. In spite of everything, in spite of what had been her daily reality for all these years, this was her daughter. Maybe she had taken this latest lesson to heart. Maybe the two of them could stay together a while longer.

"I'll get the brush," Muriel said, her stoicism a sort of kindness.

So she took the brush from the crude shelf and sat on the bed again, and made her face a stone while she removed the hood and combed out her daughter's long white hair.

5

LOLA CINCHED her robe and announced breakfast. Ross smiled, as he had every morning for a week, and closed his eyes again. He turned over into the middle of the bed, luxuriating in the space. Their involvement had deepened dramatically in the short time they'd spent together, though neither wanted to push too fast.

In the meantime, she had taken up country music (of which he was not wildly fond), and he had taken up reading popular fiction. He even read on the job, during long dull stretches spent at the station house.

Succumbing to the cooking smells, Ross finally roused himself and, donning one of her housecoats, shuffled out to the kitchen.

"Very becoming," she said as he slumped into a chair at the table, his hair slightly wild, eyes squinty.

"I thought I asked for a six A.M. wake-up," he said, yawning. "It can't even be five-thirty."

"I don't recall being hired as your private alarm clock," she teased. "Besides, you don't need sleep. You're in love."

"Man, that smells good." He sighted the coffee pot at his cup with one eye closed, and poured.

She doled out his eggs, just the way he liked them, and white toast. "Rough night?" she inquired with a sarcastic smile.

"Sublime," he said and sipped his black coffee.

"Are you available for some chauffeur work later?" she said, joining him at the table with her own plate and cup. He watched her pour coffee for herself.

"You still want to drive out there." It was not really a question.

She nodded. "Yes. I told you. I'm not giving up on her."

"Nobody's asking you to. It's just that maybe we should take along a trained professional."

Lola fell silent.

"Lola, you've got those photographs of her at six. I mean, what did your people think?"

She kept her gaze on her plate and shrugged as naturally as she could, but it wasn't easy. The department didn't know; she hadn't officially notified anyone. Nor had they seen the graphic evidence of MaryAnn Nelson's tragedy.

It had taken her a long time to open the envelope. At first she argued with herself, and with him, that it was an invasion of the child's privacy, that they had no right. But she had eventually admitted, at least to herself, the hollowness of the argument. She was putting off the inevitable, enjoying her burgeoning relationship with Ross, and nightly closing her dresser drawer on the envelope and the situation. She had opened it impulsively one morning when she realized the school term was rushing by and the chance slipping away for the state of Georgia to do right by MaryAnn Nelson. Still, there were moments when she wished she hadn't unsealed the envelope, had never gotten herself into this situation, although she could barely admit it.

She realized too late that showing Ross the polaroids had been a mistake. The pictures, crude as they were, had unnerved him also. The face distorted like some hideous clown's. The skin wooly, head high-domed, forehead flat, the lips misshapen and drawn back on one side, exposing the teeth that looked more like fangs than human dentition. This was not just a deformed kid, he had argued, although he had never seen the kids she had managed to mainstream into the school system back home. Yes, this was someone with an extreme infirmity, but Lola Aragon wasn't walking away.

Ross fussed with his toast and tried again. "You know, I really think this is a matter for the Child Services Bureau."

She said nothing.

He said, "I mean, we don't have a court order or any kind of official backing. We could be stirring up a hornet's nest by showing up at this woman's house without being fully prepared for all the possible contingencies."

She made a noncommital noise.

"What do you say we stop by Child Services and talk to somebody about this case?" He smiled at her.

"You don't *have* to help me, Ross Walker," she said sternly. "It's my responsibility and I intend to go, even if I have to get there on a motorcycle."

"Aw, hell, Lola. You know I'm not trying to get out of driving you out there. I just think we should turn this over to someone with experience in this kind of problem."

"I can handle it."

"We suspect the mother is a headcase, and it's almost a sure bet that the girl is beyond any help we could give her."

"'Almost,'" she said.

He made a helpless gesture, waving the silverware. "I don't want to abandon her. I only want to have somebody from Child Services to direct the matter."

Lola wiped her mouth and tossed the checkered napkin alongside her plate. "Look, you know very well what that involves—weeks, maybe months of paperwork, lots of meetings to decide if there's a legitimate reason for investigating, and then a committee consensus on the preliminary recommendation, maybe even a legal review." She gave a dismissive wave. "MaryAnn Nelson will be twenty-one before they scrape the rust from their various decision making bodies. I have the legal authority to check all the details of her situation on my own, now, and that's what I'm going to do."

His eyes flashed. "Then I hope you're prepared to walk dead cold into the situation out there, because I don't think I am, and one of us has to be."

"I am."

"Good. But I'm telling you. You've seen the pictures. She was six then. She's almost a woman now, an adult coming into her full powers. You've never dealt with anybody who was out of his head."

"You don't know she's crazy."

"And you don't know she isn't. Hell, she might even be a basket case unable to care for herself. That's why we need someone trained to go out there with us."

"You're the expert, I suppose," she snapped.

He paused over his plate.

"I'm sorry, Ross," she said.

He forced a smile. "Look, once we go in, it's official. The wheels go in motion and you no longer have all that much control. I'm just worried we'll blunder in and say and do all the wrong things, maybe have to remove her, maybe do her more harm than good."

Lola leaned closer across the table. "Honey, I can't wait around to see how it all works out by itself. Physical deformity makes no statement about the value of a person. And I certainly can't go by local superstition and half-assed stories about her flying around the county on a broomstick. My job is to protect the interests of kids. The damn county apparatus had its chance. They haven't done anything in sixteen years. They turned their backs and wished it would go away. And now you're telling me to involve them and go slow. I won't."

DEPUTY JAMES Lowell lifted the brim of his hat and wiped a sleeve across his forehead. It was barely daylight and already in the 80s. Crazy weather. By midday it would be a downright scorcher. He didn't want to be out in the middle of nowhere at the noon hour and resigned himself to pacing the imaginary grid he had laid out going north from the spot where the car had been. Checking his watch he headed out. He would go north for four minutes, then east for four, south for four, back to the beginning spot. He would step a few paces east and set out for another circuit, each time reducing the perimeter so that eventually he would cover the entire grid. Another couple of hours and he'd be out of there. The grass and twigs swished and snapped as he pushed through; at least nothing was going to sneak up on him in these woods. The sun baked red soil was already hard again, rain and all.

A motorist had reported the junked car a day earlier and Deputy Dorothea Winston had been dispatched. Seeing the rental plates, she had jumped to conclusions right away, and she was right. Fingerprints, lifted from the steering wheel and glove compartment, matched the female found at the dump. A computer check with the Miami PD showed no warrants outstanding on her. Notification was initiated inter-state to bring the news to her kin, if any. The car rental agency records further confirmed the female's ID; she'd paid with a Visa Gold Card. End of story.

Nothing of this was released to the papers, and the interest of Duncan County's citizens in the unsolved double homicide remained nominal. The victims were not county residents, so folks felt the killings didn't really involve their community. James Lowell chortled. To their minds the murders had only technically occurred in Duncan, especially since the bodies had been found near the county line. He was glad of it, too, because the lack of public interest reduced the pressure on the lawmen assigned to the case, and the pursuit assumed a more rational routine than if the two had been locals. Part of the drill, of course, had included a thorough search of the location at which the car had been recovered.

Lowell had been delegated the secondary search: a pro forma walk-through, really, as the site had been pretty well chewed up by the "talcum troop" from the forensics office at the Winfield barracks, and then by the tow truck. That, and the recent rain, left little hope for anything interesting to come out of his clambering around in the weeds and brush. But orders were orders and dutifully he had driven out again to the spot on the highway marked as the place where the rental car and its occupants had left the road forever.

Maintaining a straight line was hard, what with all the underbrush and pines he had to detour around. Looking at his watch, he saw he had another minute to trek before turning ninety degrees east. At thirty seconds, he counted down. At "one" he stopped. The last thirty or forty feet had taken him onto a small, unwooded rise. He pivoted to gaze back down to the road but couldn't see it through the trees he had passed through. But he could see the knoll on the far side of the road below. It had a sharp incline of protruding rock. To the side of the rock face he thought he saw someone. Someone standing, looking back at him. He stared, and the other person stared. He or she remained immobile. "Yo," he called out. His voice echoed back. "He-llo." He waved. Nothing.

Maybe he was imagining it, maybe it was something that looked like a human outline. He lifted his hat and held it high to shield his eyes.

The shape was inanimate. The thing was a thing and not a person. Lowell turned due east, checked his watch for the next four minute installment and marched off. Sixteen minutes later he had completed the route, stepped off five paces east from where he had begun and walked north again. And so it went for the next hour. The only thing he found was a used picture postcard, a black-and-white picture, tinted blue, of the Folkston Motel. The fine print on the back enumerated the attractions: 27 comfortable units, free TV, snack bar and swimming pool (seasonal). It had nothing to do with anything but he dutifully deposited it in a clear plastic bag and secured his find in the outside band of his hat. Then he adjusted his schedule for the elapsed time and pressed on.

Pausing at the northernmost point of his sixth circuit, he looked again at the knoll on the other side of the road. Oddly, the shape was gone. But then the angle had changed and, no doubt, the terrain had blocked his view.

By noon he had completed his duty. The tarmac was bubbling. He should have gotten in his car and enjoyed an air-conditioned ride back to the station. But the shape among the rocks of the knoll bothered him, even though he wasn't certain why. Still, he trusted his instincts enough to go have a closer look.

Crossing the road, he stepped into the treeline. Fifteen feet in, he paused and squatted down . . . and listened. The woods were camouflage green and full of memories. Something on the knoll had elicited them. He listened for several minutes, took off his hat, hung it on a branch. There were no sounds other than the usual murmur of wind and the warble of the odd bird. He rose very quietly and drew his side arm, then continued up, all the while listening and watching.

The climb was steep but the rocks allowed for good footing. Just short of the top there was a break between boulders and he slipped through into a rocky limestone chimney. Now the way up was noisier as pebbles came loose and cascaded down. He cursed but there was nothing to be done. After a short climb, he came out somewhere behind the top of the boulders. It was like a natural grotto, lush with ferns and newly budded leaves. In one corner stood the thing he must have seen from the other rise. It was fascinating and repellent at the same time.

It was the tall stump of a white pine maybe eleven feet high. It had hair. He went closer. The hair was made of dried weeds and braided vines; it appeared to flow away into the surrounding trees, the mock hair seeming to float, wheeling around the head. Two thick but supple branches had been pulled together in front and tied, then carved into cupped hands that held a skull of some kind. It was the size of a dog's but oddly shaped. Whorls of fur flowed from the ear cavities. The torso was scaly and pierced all over by wooden fish, fish with bared teeth, like perch, eyes round, unlidded. It was shot through with these—or had they eaten through? The thing looked like a totem done up by a loco Indian.

The head was hard to make out. Unlike the rest of it, the features looked half finished. Or maybe a hiker'd had at it. Someone had hacked into it, so that it looked like a wild boar's head, the nose truncated into a snout, making the eyeteeth look like tusks or fangs.

6

THE WIPERS squeaked on the windshield. Ross and Lola could hardly have picked a worse day. The morning was cold, windy and drizzly. The sky looked like frosted glass.

As they left Sturgis, heading northwest, the two talked about the three films they had already seen that week, where to have dinner Sunday night, the book Ross had recently read—anything but where they were going and what awaited them there. Lola rummaged in her bag and brought out a thick, worn paperback.

"Almost forgot," she said. "More for you to immerse yourself in."

"I'm so immersed now, I feel like should be wearing my library card on my chest when I sit down at my duty desk instead of my badge."

"It's nice to know our tax dollars are going to support industrious and enlightened public servants."

"He also serves who sits and answers the telephone," Ross said.

"What better way to keep your mind from turning into tomato sauce than by reading a good book?" Lola glanced at the unbroken rank of trees that lined the road. "We're getting closer," she said.

Ross nodded, eyes on the road. They had left behind other traffic and all houses. For miles there had been no signs of settlement aside from the pavement and scant telephone lines.

"You sure have a lot of trees," she said, looking out.

"Yep. More than half the state is forested: twenty-four million acres. More timber than anywhere else in the country, except for Oregon and Washington. Not much out here except the interstate."

"You up to this, Ross?" she said.

"Huh? What do you mean?"

"You seem preoccupied."

"Hadn't noticed. Must be tired."

"Something on your mind?"

He looked over at her. "Lola, if this girl's mom answers our questions, and we see that the girl is alive and okay and not in any immediate danger, then I think we should go back and take it through official channels."

"We've had this conversation before. This is no time to be timid."

"And it's no time to blunder. There's nothing to be gained, crashing into somebody's life that we know next to nothing about. If we wind up dragging this poor kid out of there without the proper preparation, we could do a lot of damage.

I just don't want us to make the situation worse. You see my point?"

Lola was uneasy. "If I said the word, you'd turn around and forget the whole thing right now, wouldn't you?"

He didn't look directly at her but could sense the expression in her angry eyes. The car became very quiet.

Ross didn't know the exact location of the Nelson house, but he had established, at the records department, that this was the road on which Muriel Nelson maintained a mailbox at the turnoff to her home. Just when he had spotted a chain link fence and the mailbox, the sky opened and it poured.

"Damn," he mumbled, and eased the car to a stop in front of the mailbox with the faded name on it that read something Nelson. Then he turned into the muddy driveway and braked before the gate.

"I don't see a house," Lola said.

"It's a huge lot she's got. If the house is set to the rear, it could be a mile or more back in the trees."

"Completely isolated. Well, what now, Kojak?"

"Let's hope they're not so far in the woods that they can't hear this." He sounded the car horn for three, four, five seconds. Then they waited. A minute went by without response. He tried again, pressing the horn for a full twenty seconds. The rain slacked off and stopped. Nobody showed.

"Let's show 'em we mean business," he said and hit the police siren. It's wail curled out over the woodlands and back. "Hah," he said.

"Phase Two?" Lola suggested.

Ross switched the radio setting to the loudspeaker and keyed the microphone. *"Muriel Nelson . . . this is Deputy*

Sheriff . . . Ross Walker . . . of the Duncan County Sheriff's office. This is official. Kindly open your gate."

They waited. Ross switched off the engine and rolled down the window. Lola rolled down hers, too. Minutes passed.

"Nothing and nobody," she said. "Does this mean we'll have to get a warrant and break down the fence?"

Ross exhaled. "Normally that would be the way to handle it. But—don't let this get around—the law still gives us a couple of other options."

"Such as?"

"First, we're here on county business. Next, the lot isn't posted. I haven't seen a 'No Trespassing' sign, have you?"

She shook her head.

"And, since neither the woman or the girl has been seen in some time, it's within my powers, as duly appointed officer of the law, to choose to investigate their current states of health."

Lola sat up, cheered. "Do you shoot off the lock?"

"You're really taken with us quiet men of action, aren't you?" he said. "Can you drive this bucket of bolts? I'm going to courageously forge a path through that slop out there."

"The car?" she said. "Me?"

"Yep."

"Well, sure . . . I guess. Why?"

"When I crack the gates, ease it through. I'll close them behind us."

"All right, if you won't get into trouble letting an un-authorized civilian operate an official vehicle."

"Hey, I'm breaking into private property. What's another charge." He turned the ignition and re-started the engine.

"Don't tease," Lola said, and poked at him as he slid out. "I hate stick shifts."

"I'll tell the sheriff." Pulling on his cap, he stepped out into the misty drizzle, while she slid across and settled behind the steering wheel. He hadn't worn his rain gear because he had trusted himself to predict the weather. Dead wrong, as usual, he thought. The cold wet cut through him as as stepped into it and he sucked a tight breath through his teeth. Come on RW, he told himself, be tough. Show her that a Southern boy can take a little cool weather. The water was soaking through his half boots as he slogged through pools to the gate.

It was a simple looking lock, built into the gate, with a slot opening that allowed it to be turned from either side. He slipped his key ring from beneath the edge of his jacket and fumbled through the huge collection, his fingers slick. Selecting a likely looking master, he slid the key into the lock and twisted. It refused to turn. He selected another and tried again. It clicked with a sweet sound.

There didn't seem to be any kind of alarm device, so he pushed open both sides of the gate and motioned for Lola to drive through. She waved back and put the patrol car in gear. It made a grinding sound and lurched forward, engine roaring, splashing him as it went by. From the knees down, he was soaked.

He shook his head and muttered as he closed one half of the gate and then the other. Then he walked to the car. Lola was already manuevering past the shift stick.

"Sorry," she said, as he took the wheel.

He forced a smile and eased the car forward, up the dirt track. He drove slowly along the ruts. Reaching the treeline, they entered a tunnel-like grove of pine and dogwood that lessened the light and turned it a bluish tone. It felt like they were inside something—another place, far from anything. Except for brief clear breaks, covered with tall grass, the canopy of towering trees claimed the road.

"No electrical lines," he said. "No telephone wires."

A large bird, an owl, vaulted off a branch directly overhead and swooped along the alley of trees, its wings gigantic looking as it flapped and soared, then vanished upward.

"Yeah, you're right," she said. "I don't see any power lines. I wonder how they get their electricity."

"Maybe they don't. Not every nook and corner in the state is electrified."

"That probably can be said of any rural area in the country. No need for y'all to get defensive."

"'Y'all' is never singular, ma'am. Only second person plural. We're not a bunch of barefoot, racist, inter-bred idiots like the national media likes to portray us. And we observe the rules of grammar, too."

She said, "It still seems unlikely to me that someone with a lot this size would have a house without electricity."

"Probably has a generator."

"Well," she said with mild indignation, "why did you wait so long to bring up that possibility." She peered ahead, down the lane of trees looming over them, around them. "I feel like Gretel. Didn't Endicott say that she had a telephone for a while?"

"Yeah, sixteen years back. Until she quit paying the bills."

"Where are those lines do you suppose?"

"Long gone," he said and eased the vehicle around a rut. Tufts of weeds and even saplings brushed against the bottom of the car.

"Some road," he said. "This is like being inside a snare drum."

"The lady really takes her privacy seriously," Lola said.

He sneezed. "She's had her reasons."

They topped a muddy hill at a crawl and saw the house, or what was left of it. It had once been a fair-sized place, judging from the dimensions of the stone foundation. Probably it had had three bedrooms, maybe a den and a dining room, bath, sitting room. But it was far from its original state. Half of it, at least, had been burned to the ground at one time. The evidence of this was the gaping black wound facing them. The other half was damaged, too, but still stood, crudely repaired in places with rough boards and logs chinked with mud and clay. The roof had been similarly patched everywhere. It wasn't much: maybe three or four remaining rooms above a hillside basement. Most of the windows had been replaced by rough-cut squares of plywood and cardboard. How, Lola wanted to know, did they get sunlight? They didn't, Ross explained, but the absence of working windows conserved heat in winter.

As they rolled closer, they made out a small wooden hut, no larger than a doghouse, set on the far side of the place. Ross identified it as the covering to the well. A crude looking outhouse could be seen in the trees a little ways down the slope.

Facing the house, set further back, in what had once been a small clearing, was a small solid barn. No livestock were visible anywhere. A handful of fruit trees around the barn appeared long unpruned and uncultivated. In the earth of the basement in the destroyed half of the house was a vegetable gardened walled in by the foundation stones. The car rolled to a stop ten paces from the lone door.

Lola was incredulous. "Not even gingerbread. Can anyone live in that?"

"Lola," he said, "these are poor, hard folk. They're not like anybody you've run into so far."

"What are you saying?"

"Go slow, go easy. Get a sense of them. These are people living on gristle."

"I didn't exactly grow up on Peachtree Lane, Deputy."

"Yeah, but you had a telephone, a TV, VCR, a washer-dryer— down at the launderette at least. These people— "

Dogs bounded out of the forest and set themselves about the car, barking and wailing like sentries—three huge Dobermans, black, slick with rain. And a fierce German shepherd.

"Well," Ross said in a jaunty tone. "We're here."

"Forget it. I'm not leaving this car while those things are out there."

The lone door opened and a gaunt woman with brown and gray hair stepped into the doorway. She was wearing a shabby dress and a shotgun, and a very perturbed expression.

"Our hostess," Ross said, and rolled down his window just enough to be heard. "Miss Nelson?"

"What do you want?" the woman said. "Who are you?"

"The car should be a clue," he said to Lola, then more loudly, "I'm Deputy Walker, Miss Nelson. Duncan County Sheriff's Department. This is official, so you just put that gun away, ma'am."

Muriel didn't appear impressed. "Get off my property," she said and gestured with the barrel.

"I can't do that, ma'am. I'm asking you in a calm, respectful manner to put up the gun." His shirt stuck to his back along his spine. "Nobody's here to harm you."

"You've got no call being here."

"Miss Nelson, I am a representative of the law, and that means I have business where I say I have business. Now, put that shotgun away and call off these animals."

The stronger tone worked. Muriel Nelson pondered for the briefest moment, the conflict clear in her weathered face, but finally propped the weapon inside her doorway. With two fingers in her mouth and tongue curled, she whistled like a commuter catching a cab and the four baying dogs immediately shut up and faced her.

"Pen, pen!" she ordered and they raced away, around the house, out of sight. The woman turned back to Ross and Lola, stepping closer. "What do you want?"

Ross opened his door and stepped into the light rain. "We'd like to come inside and talk to you."

Muriel motioned to the car. "Who's she?"

"That's Dr. Aragon, head of the county Educational Services. She's requested this meeting."

Muriel muttered, "That's it, I guess," then raised her chin to them. "Come on then."

Ross walked around to the passenger side of the car, just in case the dogs decided to reappear. Lola had on rain gear and boots, but she still hurried across the muddy yard to the door.

When she and Ross were inside, Muriel said, "Okay, I don't have all day to waste."

Lola mumbled, staring at her surroundings. The only light was from the open door. It was hot and musty. The large room was completely filled with old furniture, cord wood, wood sculptures of no definite form, a milk crate full of car batteries, two jerry cans of kerosene, the hose and bulb of a gasoline syphon, a half-dozen fan belts hanging on a peg, a box of tools and wrenches, large slabs of cardboard and huge rolls of paper that looked like photographers' backdrops, a bedspring and mattress mounted on milk crates, and countless boxes of books. Hardbound, paperbound, spiral bound—they were everywhere. Even the long Empire sofa was covered with them.

"Mrs. Nelson," Lola said.

"Miss."

"Yes . . . Miss Nelson. I . . . ."

"I guess," Muriel said, her voice amused, "I guess I should offer you a seat. Clear off a place somewhere and sit."

Ross knew that he should take command of the situation, impose himself as the confident authority. But it was difficult to do as he found himself shifting dusty boxes to the floor to clear a space for himself and Lola, and then sitting down on the horsehair sofa as if it were commonplace to face a hearth gerry-rigged with suspended cooking pots and a grating to serve as a stove, and to be flanked by teetering boxes piled to eye-level. Lola, next to him, was taking it all in, dwarfed by the detritus stacked up next to her. Muriel remained standing, making it even more uncomfortable. Command presence, he thought, and gave it a try.

"Let's get straight to it, then, Miss Nelson," he said. "We've come about your daughter."

"What about her?"

Lola leaned forward, her posture blunt. "Is she alive?"

Muriel snorted and gazed coolly at them. "Yes."

"Could we speak to her, please?"

"She doesn't talk to people. She doesn't like to be seen."

"We may have to insist on it," Lola said.

Muriel Nelson looked uninterested.

Ross said, "Why haven't you ever enrolled her in school? State law requires that you do so, you know."

"You can't be serious," Muriel replied.

"Ma'am, we need to establish that she . . . has survived."

"Where," Lola said, "is MaryAnn now?"

"Behind you."

Lola turned abruptly. There was no one.

Muriel, smiling, pointed. "In her room, there." It was the large door to what once would have been the parlor.

Swallowing, Lola quickly said, "Would you call her out here? Since this is about her, she should take part, don't you think?"

Muriel pushed a book onto the floor and sat down in a straight-backed chair, amidst her eccentric possessions.

"Miss Nelson?" Lola said. "I asked you— "

"Forget it, honey. Unless you show me some kind of warrant, this is the limit of the cooperation you'll get from me. My daughter is asleep. I'm not having you disturb her."

Ross saw she wasn't bluffing. They hadn't served her with anything and she had correctly sized it up as a fishing expedition. He caught the top of a pile of books about to topple on him and righted it, taking the top-most one away. It was an encyclopedia from maybe the 50s. Giving out a resigned sigh, he said to Lola, "Let's get on with it, Dr. Aragon."

Lola took over. "Once more then," she said. "Why haven't you allowed MaryAnn to receive schooling?"

Muriel Nelson laughed bitterly. "Why do all the kids in the county sing mean little ditties about 'The Spook'? Why did they break out our windows with rocks eight years back, and burn down half my house before I got the guard dogs? Why is everyone afraid to come within five miles of this place after dark? Why has it taken the county ten years to get around to us" — she paused — "if the county's *really* interested? What the county *really* would have preferred is for us to just go away, or up and die. What the county *really* is, is inconvenienced."

Ross sat silent, nervously flipping pages of the encyclopedia. Lola said, "If it's due to her physical problems —"

"Problems?" Muriel parroted. "Girl, haven't you talked to your new neighbors. That child is the handmaiden of Satan."

"Miss Nelson," Lola whispered. "Please. She might overhear."

Muriel snorted. "Don't you think she knows what she is? She's had fifteen years of abuse by her *normal* peers and their ever-so-normal parents. And you imply I've mistreated her by not allowing her to go out among you sanctimonious . . . ."

"Ma'am," Ross said, "we're not here to accuse you of anything. The law says —"

"The law!" she said. "Everything's the law with you, isn't it? As far as I'm concerned, you can just shove your law up a dark hole."

Ross colored but didn't respond. He put aside the encylopedia and took up flipping through a second volume beneath it, distancing himself from the confrontation, the responsible professional who was remaining objective and dispassionate, doing his pro forma duty in trying to reason with an impossibly obstinate citizen.

Lola said, "If she's mentally accountable, there are special schools she can attend. And there may be additional options, like reconstructive surgery or — "

"Which takes money, just like your damn schools take money. Do I look like a millionaire? Would I be living here if I was?"

"If it's just a question of money, I'm sure that there are foundations we can contact. And, surely, there's enough heart in this community to set up a fund. She can't stay hidden in the shadows, like some misbegotten object of divine punishment. You can't keep your child ignorant."

Muriel Nelson sat rigid. "I'm not a charity case, and I won't let you turn her into one."

Lola looked down at her hands, then up into the lined, taut face of Nedra Muriel Nelson. "Are you so ashamed of having borne her that you can't stand to let her have a life of her own. Is it her physical problem, or your pride?"

Muriel's lips curled in a sneer. "My God, how perceptive of you. You've discovered my real motives."

Lola's face went pale.

"I'm protecting her," Muriel said. "I always have. And I am keeping her and looking after her . . . the best I can. She has nothing to worry about, long as I'm alive."

"And after you?" Lola said. "Who'll take over?"

Muriel Nelson did not answer.

"Or are you planning to live forever?"

"Nobody . . ." said Muriel, staring hard, "lives forever. Nobody loves forever. Who out there is going to love her? Marry her? Look after her? Who are you kidding? I'm her mother and I wish sometimes she was never born. And when she was, I wished that she'd die. Wished I'd held her head in the toilet."

Lola's eyes were wide with disbelief.

"Not pretty to hear. I know, girl. I bore her. You'd best pray that you never have to be the kind of mother I've been. What's the matter, shocked? Or has your high, moral indignation deserted you? Easy to plan your attack on a crazy woman and her freak kid, yes? Not so easy to have to listen to what it's really like to live with this. Were you expecting to hear all about the melodramatic self-sacrifice?" She sniffed. "The county elders are kind of late with their concern, but they can rest easy in their beds tonight. We're not going anywhere. They can't take her away from me. She's been my burden and my responsibility all her life, and you can't just prance your high asses in here and take her."

"It's not our job to take her anywhere," Ross said. "But we are reporting back to people who have the legal duty to look out for children like MaryAnn."

"Right, you're just the errand boy. Well, let me tell you. If the county moves to take her, I'll countersue for malfeasance, dereliction of duty, violation of civil rights, injury and damages for the county's failure to act for all this time. You want to bring us out into the lovely light? Ha. Your mayor and county board will be quaking for decades. Some liberal lawyer will have a field day, making his reputation. If he wins, the town won't be repairing any sewers for a lot of years. And my daughter and I will have enough of the county's money to build a Berlin Wall around this place. Not that you'll be around to see it. They'll have suspended your asses by then, for starting all this in the first place. 'Shoulda left well enough alone,'" she said, mimicking. "So *don't* you two go threatening me!"

There was a small squeaking sound, something striking wood—or being yanked from it, Ross thought. Like a log creaking closed when the blade pulls free. The sound had come from behind the closed door.

Muriel stiffened. "I think this matter is settled. So why don't you and your boyfriend get out of here."

"Shut up," Lola said very calmly. She got up and walked past Muriel Nelson to the door of MaryAnn's room. A large bolt was in place, an old fashioned lock alongside it. The girl was locked in! She turned around. "We need to talk to her, Miss Nelson. We need to establish for ourselves that she is alive."

Muriel sat sideways in the chair, looking at Lola Aragon. She could see the woman was weighing whether to undo the door.

"I hope you're not thinking of violating the law, lady. As the deputy will tell you, you have no right to violate my home. I don't want you to go in there."

Lola stared at the knob for a moment. What would it take to slide away the bolt and breach that child's isolation?

"Please—" Muriel Nelson said in an exaggerated tone, clearly for the record.

"Look," Ross said from behind them. He was standing by the fireplace, a magazine in his hand. He plopped it atop the fan belts in the wooden milk crate and stepped around the box of car batteries. "Miss Nelson, we have to know she's okay. That's all. Otherwise I've got to go to that car and radio in for more officers to help investigate immediately."

Muriel rose. She looked haggard. "Okay. Okay, you can talk to her. She pushed past Lola to the door and pounded on it with the heel of her fist. "MaryAnn!"

There was no answer.

"MaryAnn. Answer me. I know you've been listening."

Ross and Lola exchanged looks.

"Yes, ma'am." The voice was soft, muffled.

"You've been listening," Muriel said. "Is that right? Tell the truth."

"Yes, ma'am."

"Speak up," Muriel said, "so we can hear you."

There was an odd clinking sound—links cascading to the floor. Lola shot Ross a look. Was the girl *chained* in there?

Muriel leaned her head against the wall by the door, eyes shut. "There are some people out here who are very concerned about you. They think maybe I've been neglecting you all these years, and that you're stupid and can't read, or say your numbers." She paused. "Are you stupid?"

There was a long silence. Muriel looked up, glaring at the door.

"Answer me!"

The only response was a small cough. Muriel looked back at her visitors. "She's not used to speaking to strangers. MaryAnn?" She turned again to the door. "What do you have to say?"

"I don't know, Mama," the voice said. "I . . . I'm not too smart, I guess. But you taught me, Mama. I can read some."

"Miss Nelson," Lola said, staring at the profile of Muriel Nelson. "You don't have to put her through this."

"Tell us the months of the year. And spell them."

"There are qualified people who would be able to evaluate her and determine what help she needed."

"January. Capital J-A-N-U-A-R-Y." The voice was tremulous.

Lola's embarrassment for the child was profound. "Miss Nelson," she whispered.

"February. F-E-B-R-U-A-R-Y. March . . . ."

Hands in her pockets, Lola paced back toward Ross, standing with elbow resting on a box piled high with moldy books. The recitation continued. Ross flipped open the book next to his elbow and motioned to it with his chin. Lola looked quizzical, then went closer.

"June. J-U-N-E . . . ."

Lola looked at the page casually held open. It was a sixth grade geography. The margins were all decorated with elaboate designs. Not the dreamy doodles of young imaginations. These were determined, definite lines forming figures that were like symbols. At first she thought that was what he had wanted to show her, but then she saw something else. A halftone photographic illustration. It was of tribesmen somewhere in Asia. The faces were obliterated, marked out in black. Ross flipped the pages slowly. The leaves tumbled past in a slow cadence, revealing blacked out faces wherever there were photos of people, page after page, face after face.

"December. D-E-C-E-M-B-E-R."

"Let's try mathematics," Muriel said.

Lola rolled her eyes at Ross. "Miss Nelson."

"Subtract three hundred and sixty-two from seven hundred and eighteen."

"Can I use a pencil, Mama?"

"Please," Lola said forcefully.

Muriel Nelson nodded. "All right, MaryAnn. Forget it."

"I think I can do it without a pencil, Mama. I think I—"

"Shut up!" Muriel said. "These people out here think that you'd be better off if they put you in some kind of special school. And then maybe they'll put you in a hospital and make you look better. How would you like to go with them?"

"No."

"Wouldn't you like that?"

"Please! I don't want to go, Mama. Don't let them cut me."

Something walloped the door—hard. Lola jumped back.

Muriel smiled. "What? I can't hear you."

"You said you'd never make me go away, Mama. You promised!"

Lola touched his arm. "Ross."

He stepped to the door. "That will do, Miss Nelson. Tell her everything is fine, and that we haven't come to take her from you."

"Ever?" she said.

"Miss Nelson."

"You're about as tough as wet bread, Deputy," she said, with evident pleasure. "All right, MaryAnn. Calm down."

"People will laugh at me," the girl cried out. "They'll hurt me with rocks. Please, let me stay, Mama. I promise I won't do terrible things anymore."

Muriel banged the door with her palm. "Shut the hell up!"

"I'll read a book for them! Do you want me to show them?"

"*Shut up*," Muriel screamed. "You do what I tell you to or I'll let them take you right now!"

The voice went dead silent. The rain came down harder.

Muriel looked at them. "You see what your 'help' does? It

drives her into hysterics. She's just fifteen. She's scared to death of what's out there."

"You weren't fair," Lola said.

"Fair? She was almost burned to death when she was eight. For all the years before that, high school kids would prowl around, sneaking looks and trying to taunt her. They made it part of their club initiations. Fucking little creeps stalking her at night, painted up for their ceremonies, one dressed like an infant in diapers."

"You haven't exactly helped the situation," Lola said.

Muriel's look was venomous. "Why don't you just go. Leave us. Or are you two trying for some kind of award? Okay, consider yourselves heroes, but you'd better know that we're better off without your goddamned interference. So you and your do-good friends stay away from us."

"Miss Nelson, you're an adult. You can ruin your own life if you want to. You don't have the right to do it to hers."

"You don't know," Muriel said.

"I do know. I saw the pictures you provided the board. I saw a human being, not a creature to be locked away. I don't give a damn if she is your child. You can't deny her education. You don't have a right to deny her the opportunity to use her mind and to have the courage to make a life."

"You should run for office, lady. Or is this already part of your campaign to enliven the sluggish Southerners?"

"*Ooooooooooo.*"

Lola and Ross stepped back from the startling cry behind the door.

"Jesus," he said.

"Go squeeze out some yourself," Muriel sneered at Lola, unaffected by the sound. "Maybe you'll be lucky, too. Then we can compare notes on—what did you call it?—'divine punishment'?"

"Lola," Ross said, "she's just trying to incite. There's no more to be done here now. Let's go." He ushered Lola toward the door and out. Muriel Nelson followed. The rain cascaded off the roof and ricocheted off the brown and gold police cruiser. Lola marched toward the passenger side; Ross, hunched, padded toward the driver's.

"You've got good hips," Muriel Nelson called out, trailing after her through the muddy yard, ignoring the downpour. "You could pop them out like an old mama hog. Oooeeee," she hooted.

Lola spun around. "You bitter . . . . What you've done isn't only immoral. If you think you're going to get away with it just because she's turning sixteen, you're crazier even than you act. You're not qualified to have a pet, much less a child. You're unspeakable."

"And you're kidding yourself if you think this is just your job. This is something else for you, honey. Something that runs deep. What, huh? What? You're gonna redeem yourself by taking my child away to some institution? Are you going to love it the way I should have? What is it with you . . . Lo-la?"

The two women were faced off, standing ankle deep in mud and water.

"Listen closely, Muriel. I have good instincts, too. And I sense something here, even stranger than your sideshow. And I don't like it. What you're hiding isn't what you'd have us think it is."

"Dr. Aragon," Ross called.

They stared at one another, rivulets streaming down their noses and chins.

"Good day, Miss Nelson," Lola said, walked to the car and got in.

"Go! Go!" Muriel Nelson yelled, the muscles in her face like cords. She kicked water at the car in great fans. "Get off my land. Get!"

Ross Walker revved the engine and reversed, then put it in gear and pulled away, slowly, back down the canopied tunnel of evergreens and maples.

Muriel Nelson followed, hurling sticks and epithets, kicking at the puddled water. When the car was no longer visible, she went around to the back and unloosed the dogs.

ROGER CASEY dreamed. It was like a dream he had had once before, his sleeping mind noted. He was walking through a long corridor with no doors. He began to run. The concussion of every footfall did something to him. The sensation was intense, wonderful. At the end of the tunnel was a slight rise, where she waited.

She had on a white shift with red raked across it, her back to him. Her legs looked hollow, her arms translucent. When she turned to face him, his throat swelled shut.

She drew him and he flew to her. Their limbs locked, faces brow to brow. His body lunged into her and burst.

LOLA AWOKE gasping. It was a moment before she realized it was a dream that had awoken her. Like most dreams, it was receding fast, erasing itself in the light. Funny . . . sleep and dreams had always been a refuge. She dreamed frequently, vividly. This was an ugly exception. The radio-alarm clock went off filling the still air with loud and raucous music: Country and Western of the drinking and whoring variety. Charlie Daniel sang "The Devil Went Down to Georgia" one more time. She punched the OFF button and swung out of bed, took her robe and, yawning, shuffled to the kitchen, stopping on the way to run the tub for an indulgent morning bath.

Ross was in the kitchen, looking ill. "Can I get you some coffee?" he said.

"Mmmmm." She nodded and slumped into the chair across from him. He looked like a tired and lonely child. "I didn't hear you come in. Are you all right? You look so pale."

"Yeah," Ross said. "I got in late. Jimmy Lowell and I stopped off at Jeremy's for a drink and now we've got Redneck Flu."

"What's that?"

"Hangover."

"Oh."

"We didn't eat dinner during our shift. We got too busy with a traffic accident south of town. And then we drank like we were high school kids again." He shook his head, painfully. "Jeremy, too. He kept buyin' rounds. We were knockin' 'em back pretty good—Manhattans. He wanted to know where the hot little Mexican number was that he'd seen me in there with."

She stared at his plate, her face screwed up. "What are you eating?"

"He said she had a classy chassis."

"What is that stuff?" She pointed at his food.

"Just a little something I nuked in the microwave."

"Ugh," she said, making a face.

"I'm reporting for duty as soon as I finish eating and clean up a little. I gotta keep moving or I'll nose-dive right here on your kitchen floor. I feel like a gallon bucket of paint diluted with five gallons of thinner."

"Who drove home?"

"Jeremy's bartenders took me and Jimmy. It was that or sleep it off in the car behind the K-Mart."

"What was Jimmy Lowell celebrating."

"He had a religious experience out in the woods."

"Ah ha," she said, looking unconvinced. "Is that iced coffee?"

"Dr. Pepper."

She rose and went to pour herself coffee.

"You still upset?" he said.

She glanced back at him as she poured. "Yes." She added milk and stirred absently. She was tired, too.

"Everything will be all right," he said. "I really think she'll be okay until Child Services can get on it."

Lola shook her head. "She could be dead by then."

"I don't think so. You know, that shotgun? It wasn't even loaded. The breech was open and I could see it wasn't when I passed it going in."

"Great! Maybe she's out of shells. Then—if Muriel has to strangle the girl or poison her food or burn the rest of the house down while her daughter's locked away inside—maybe she'll think twice about it before going to all that trouble."

"Honey," he said, "short of going back there and slapping cuffs on her for what she might do, or might be thinking about, just what is it you'd have me do?"

"I don't know." Lola rejoined him at the table. "Maybe everyone would have been better off if I'd never gotten us involved. We certainly cranked up the mother."

"No, you were right from the start," Ross said. "Something like this doesn't fix itself. For all her alleged sophistication, Muriel Nelson isn't coping with her daughter's problems. She's buried herself and her child out there."

Lola looked wistful, worried. "Do you think they'll help her?"

"If they've got a brain among them, they will. Once it's judged an abuse case, Child Services doesn't even need a court order. We gave them first hand information." He put aside his fork and knife. "Look . . . it's not open and shut. The conditions they're living in may be brutal, but somebody can argue that it's not illegal to be dirt poor. Locking the girl up, however, constitutes abuse, illegal incarceration and the like."

"It was so depressing out there," she said.

"Yeah. I keep thinking about all those books with the faces scratched out."

"Under Georgia Law, she's not a minor much longer," Lola said. "You know that."

"Long enough." He touched her shoulder and suddenly felt closer even than when they made love. "We'll straighten out everything. I made that kid a promise."

"Me, too. Listen," she said, "my Uncle Gus has invited me to bring my boyfriend to the annual family do in New York on the Fourth of July. Can you get some time off."

"I hope he isn't a conservative minded Latino. Am I going to be interrogated about our relationship? I don't want to get you into any trouble."

"With Uncle Gus? Get serious. I had him around my finger as soon as I was able to pout."

"I think I know the look," he said, and kissed her as he made to leave.

THE AVIATOR sunglasses didn't help. Ross Walker felt like a hundred, eighty pounds of mushy cheese. Even a nothing-much day on the job was going to be an effort. In the corridor outside the Sheriff's Department office, he ran into James Lowell, who also looked several shades lighter than his usual ruddy self.

"Hi," Ross said.

"No need to scream, man."

"My condolences."

"Yeah. Mine, too. Speaking of which, the Sheriff is back from his Atlanta sojourn."

"Oh, yeah?"

"Yeah. Wants to see you first thing," Jimmy said.

"You know what about?"

"Your annual beard lecture for one. And he's royally pissed at you for taking Dr. Aragon out to the Thickets and getting the department all tangled up with Child Services. He heard you gave them a deposition and everything."

"Great." Ross bared all his teeth in a rictus grin.

"Hey, man. Watch the glare."

"Sorry."

Ross went on in and knocked on the open door of the sheriff's private office.

"Come on in, son," Sheriff Malone said. "Sit down."

The sheriff's steel-gray hair ringed his bald scalp. From the back, Jimmy Lowell said the sheriff looked like a winner's trophy cup. Ross tried not to think about the remark as he made himself comfortable in the comfortably worn leather chair alongside his boss's desk.

"Morning Mike. Good to have you back."

"Good to be back." He paused. "You know, I almost didn't recognize you when you came in just now. Stood a little far away from the razor, didn't you."

"Yes, sir. I guess I did."

"You know the regulations. Mustache is acceptable, but the rest has to go, up to your ear lobes."

"Yes, sir."

"We let you have a beard and the other fellas are going to start testing to see how far they can go, too. Hell, we might even have some of the men in earrings and the women in miniskirts, you know."

"Yes, sir."

"Want to borrow my razor before you go on duty?"

"I've got a shaving kit in my locker."

Malone leaned back in his swivel chair; the leather of the high headrest was rubbed smooth and shone like his pate. "I've got a press conference in a minute . . . 'bout the double homicide out near the line. So I'll keep this short. I understand you carried the new head of Educational Services out on a truancy case in a county squad car. That right?"

"Yes, Sheriff."

"Can't have it. I can't have you gallivanting all over the county, looking for kids who should be in school."

"There's more to it than that."

"So I understand, but I make it a point not to listen to idle gossip, especially when it's of a personal sort. If you get my meaning. Anyhow, school'll be out in a couple of months, Ross."

"The child is mentally and physically impaired, maybe incompetent, and maybe—."

"'Maybe' hell. Listen up, son. We need you on regular patrol. You can't be doin' errands for other departments. Getting minors removed from the custody of their parents is not our job. Let the child welfare people handle this."

"Yes, sir."

"Now . . . you'll have to excuse me, 'cause I've got to go tell the press how close we are to an arrest in the John and Jane Doe doubleheader."

"How close are we?" Ross said.

The sheriff grimaced. "Heck, they're still poking around the dump. Haven't even found all of 'em yet. Probably never will. We got some guesses as to why they were done in, and we have some suspicions about the victims. But that's about it. Not a clue as to who butchered 'em that way."

Ross got up. "Give 'em hell, Sheriff," he said, and left.

MARY ANN saw the lights dancing on the clouds before she actually found the place they were coming from. It reminded her of the night when the fire had burned down so much of the house, and how red the sky looked. This illumination was more white, like the color of snow. Maybe another kind of fire. She had never been this far away from the Thickets before, and was afraid she would have trouble finding her way back.

Suddenly there was a fence. It was right out in the trees. She felt the wire mesh, admired the hard wire woven into circles. Good for her toes and fingers. But she couldn't see through it. Green cloth was draped down the other side in wide strips.

MaryAnn climbed silently. At the top, her eyes rose slowly above the tarp. She looked to the lights and almost fell back down. It was like there was a hole in the sky where the sun was still shining through, even on this dark night, and there were people—giant people—in the hole above the ground. Their heads were as big as her whole house. She peeked again. There were naked heads floating in mid-air. A man's head with a beard, and a woman's, with long hair. Just heads! Their lips were moving but making no sound.

They weren't real people, of course. It must be a movie, she decided. She had never seen a movie. "Mo-vie," she said.

In front of the movie were lots of cars with their backs to her. They stood on little hills. Smells of tar and of meat reached her: ground meat like Mama cooked for her sometimes. The food odors came from a flat-topped building out in the middle of the field, the cars on either side of it and between it and the movie.

Easing gently over the top, she climbed noiselessly down the wall of loops. She moved through the black as far as she could, until she reached a large patch of light by the building. To move through light was terribly dangerous. She would never do it . . . except this was so exciting.

White metal fence posts, with boxes perched on top, emitted sounds: the voices of the movie people. A man's voice said the things that the lips of the movie man were saying. They were playing a story together. How could they pretend so well all together?

She flitted through the rectangle of light splayed across the ground, back into the shadows along the building. Her bare feet made no sound at all, except for a stone that she sent skittering. No one noticed. They were inside their cars, watching. Maybe she could get one of those radios on the white posts and take it away. A box of puffed corn lay on the ground. She loved puffed corn, loved it when Mama made it, the corn going pa-pa-pa against the lid of the pot. She stuffed some in her mouth, tasting salt and some odd oil. There was a wafer of candy. She picked it up. Things were stuck to it that she brushed off. She had had candy once, when Mama gave her some on an anniversary of her birth. Mama had gotten mad about something. MaryAnn licked off the dry grass stalks and dirt and spit them out, then pushed the wafer into her mouth. Then she noticed the small ball of candy with a stick protruding from it and did the same with it: cleaning it first, then putting it in her mouth, the stick pushing out the bottom of her hood in a funny way.

There were shrieks from the white boxes and from some of the cars. She moved quickly along the dark back wall of the building and peered around the corner. The giant people were running all about, screaming; there was smoke everywhere. Rats were pouring out of holes and across the floor of the room the people were in. Her heart was beating wildly.

"Hi," a voice said behind her. Not a box voice. Human. "Lose your car?"

She pressed closer against the wall with her back and looked at him. It was dim but not dark enough so that he couldn't see. The boy stood with white bags balanced in each hand, staring.

"This is a joke, right?"

He smiled broadly. His skin was perfect, teeth blazing white in the half-light. Eyes, too. His hair curled in a languid way, like moving water. She had never seen a young boy from so close. His neck was so slender; his head, large. He was beautiful.

She said nothing, didn't move. He seemed as rooted as she. Only his expression changed . . . ever so slowly. The lips closed around the teeth, the brow rose. She watched his jaw hinge tighten.

"I don't think you're funny. I think you're rude . . . . Why don't you say something?"

She took the lollipop from her mouth and out from under the hood. "Ooo," she said, and reached with her hand to touch his downy cheeks. So smooth. Like a rabbit's.

He moaned, stepped sideways, away from her—not turning his back on her—and tripped. The white bags struck the ground with pops, and liquids gushed out. He leapt to his feet and backed away, then vanished, feet crunching the ground rapidly as he ran.

She crossed the lighted space quickly, quietly, and trotted in the direction of the fence. Behind her she could hear more than one set of shod feet returning. She increased her pace, even though she knew they'd hear.

"Over there," called the boy's voice, angry now, confident.

She ran for the fence. They ran after her. MaryAnn leapt onto the fence, grasping the metal through the green cloth, and climbed rapidly. She was over the top in a few beats, and down the other side. Stepping away from the fence, she froze, shielded by trees and an earth rivetment.

The footfalls surged closer and slowed. Stopped.

"Holy moly, her skin was all slimey, like a frog's," she heard the beautiful boy say.

"Did you touch her? 'Cause you touched *me*. Now I gotta wash off, all over."

"Lord," said the boy. "I'll never forget it."

A kid—panting—said, "Don't you—think—we should go after—her?"

"In the woods?" the second boy said, then paused.

"Yeah, hell. Why not? Hey! Ralph. Silas. Come 'ere. We're goin' after the Spook."

"She's got a mouth like a crocodile," the beautiful boy said. "Watch it."

The youths set to scaling the fence, their bodies shadows against the green tarp, their fingers struggling for purchase through the material. MaryAnn Nelson took a large rock from the rivetment and stood to her full height. She raised it overhead and, snarling, hurled the block against the steel snare. It reverberated like a cymbal.

"Dang," someone screamed. "My hand."

With cries of alarm, they dropped back to the ground and ran for their lives.

JEREMY CARRIGAN sat on a barstool in Jeremy's Place minding his own business. Lulu sidled up to him and called out a drink order to the bartender, then said to Jeremy, "He's back again, Mr. Carrigan." She sighed. "There are a couple of guys from the hardware store on the dance floor. I'll bet they could escort him out quietly."

"No," Jeremy Carrigan said, sounding resigned. "Don't upset the patrons. No problem. We'll just have a nice chat outside."

The waitress shook her head and moved on to other customers. Nonchalantly, Jeremy sized up the would-be brawler when she moved out of his line of sight. The trouble maker was about half loaded, Jeremy estimated, but also at least six feet and well over two hundred pounds. Oh, well, he thought. The booze will slow him up. The man waddled over and parked a cheek on the stool next to his.

"You want it in here," the man said, "or outside?"

"Oh, my," Jeremy replied. The guy looked like a beetle. "That marijuana you've been sucking all night went right to your brain stem, didn't it?"

"Hey, I'm not gonna stand here all night, pop."

"Okay, okay. Let's go out back."

"After you," the man said.

"A real gentleman," Jeremy said and headed down the hall. He knew what was going to happen, of course, but he went first anyway, keeping a decent distance between himself and the oaf. It wouldn't start until both of them were out of sight of any witnesses, which meant right there in the hall, maybe five strides from the rear door. Fifteen feet from the doorway, Jeremy set his left foot and dipped from the knees. He'd been right, too. The guy was drawing back for a crunching shot to the back of the head.

Jeremy whipped his right hand back in a smooth arc and crunched the man in the groin. He shrieked and doubled over, as Jeremy pivoted into a left hook, his money punch, and connected with the guy's cheek. It was a sweet shot; Jeremy felt it all the way to his thighs, but the guy only staggered a couple of feet. Okay, the hard way, Jeremy thought. With a roar, the man threw himself at the ex-prize fighter. Despite the age difference of more than three decades, it was no contest. Jeremy slipped the guy's roundhouse punch while landing lots of his own, harder than the younger man had ever endured. A four punch combination landed the opponent right on his butt. Jeremy was only a little winded. His challenger was down for the count.

"Nicely done, boss," said the bartender, standing in the hallway's foyer with a softball bat in his hand.

"I'm too old for this," Jeremy said, catching his breath. "Look after him, will you," he said, jutting his chin at the prostrate man.

"Want me to give him a ride home?"

"Yeah." Jeremy nodded. "That would be a real public service."

"Don't give it a thought, boss. Have a good night."

The bartender called for a busboy to bring him a wet towel, and Jeremy continued down the hall to his office in the back. He let himself in and locked the door behind him.

He looked at the clock. It was eight, straight up. The familiar knock on the outside door sounded. Carrigan smiled as he walked to the door and opened it. She was standing there, as she had every week for years, unseen by anyone else.

"Come in," he said, and she did.

She walked directly to his desk and, by the time he had secured the outside door, she was naked to the waist. His breath trembled. God, how he loved the sight of her. She didn't look like any woman he had ever known. She was hard muscled, taut, and she fucked hard, too. A fighter, like him. She loosed her hair and let it tumble about her shoulders, its softness in sharp contrast to the sinewy muscles and sharply defined bones. It was all that physical labor, first as a sculptor, then as a penniless scrounger of scrap metal, wood, what have you. It was painful to think about. A hard life, yet it had its rewards. At fifty-three, Muriel Nelson had the body of an athletic thirty-year old, a body she shared with him.

He embraced her, kissed her on the neck, felt her arms go around him. He pushed at the waist of her skirt.

"I need your help," she said.

Jeremy Carrigan eased back, still holding her.

"The county's suddenly interested in my child."

He nodded.

"I'm afraid for her."

"And afraid of her?" he asked.

"No," she said. "She's my daughter."

"What are you going to do, Muriel? You can't keep her hidden away forever. She's nearly grown. She's big. Strong. How are you going to keep her? Maybe it's a good thing the county's finally gotten off its duff. Maybe they can help."

"They can't," she said. "I won't let her go."

"She's becoming a danger to herself, and maybe to other people, including you."

"No."

"They could teach her things."

"Cage her, you mean."

"Muriel."

"I won't lose her to them," she said. "I won't."

She kissed him savagely, defiantly. He realized it wasn't lust—more like rage. He kissed her back. Time was running out for them.

8

THE SHOWER was scalding. Fenton Lindsey shone red. His skin was the same bright red that the whirlpool baths had made it, back when he was still fool enough to play jock for his old man's pleasure. He tipped his head back, the hot water surging into his hair, firing his scalp. Football. What a joke. Turn your eight year old body over to a bunch of impotent former tough guys, start on steroids around twelve, rack your knees for the first time at fifteen-sixteen, then look forward to "minor" memory lapses in college, go big-time pro and hang it up at thirty-two with no legs or back and impaired kidney function, and take the one-time retirement payment quick, because the actuarial odds were that you'd be planted by sixty.

I may go young, he thought, but it'll be one hell of a sky-splitting exit. Not like some damned crippled mule that's been slapped over every square inch of his body with a baseball bat.

He laughed to himself. It hadn't even been that hard to fake the back problem. Rah-rah, zis boom bah. He'd played the game alright, and the gridiron was history. Destiny awaited. He was going to —

The phone rang, loudly enough to penetrate the drumming water. Fenton ignored it. It kept ringing.

"Son of a bitch."

He turned off the tap and stepped out. The towels were luxurious, ordered special from Rich's in Atlanta. The sex had been great. God, all afternoon, while his papa whacked divots skyward at some north Georgia golf tournament for bank presidents, and mom got her weekly whatever from the tennis pro at the club. Fenton snickered. He had caught them once in the pool, skinny dipping after one of her "lessons." That was the last time they had done it at the house.

God, he was sore, too. He had slam danced that fox all day. The phone stopped ringing, then started again almost immediately.

"All right, all right." He stalked naked into the bedroom, thinking it might actually be important, like lightning had struck his old man's five iron, or his mother's wagon had stalled on the tracks in front of an oncoming freight train.

"Hello," he half shouted.

"Fen?" It was Roger Casey. Jesus. Roger the Head, the class's evil genius. Roger Casey had been a real dude once upon a time. It had been his idea to hide on the wooded hill overlooking the county jail's exercise yard and bomb the hardasses strutting around, with firecrackers and smoke bombs and M-80s. Watching those bullshit jerks run around like a bunch of ladies when the sky started falling, was too much. And Roger had come up with the plan to lay the dead fish onto Mr.

Kolda's engine block. He had put the hidden camera in the teachers' john, too. Broke into the school and did the dirty work himself over a long weekend. Gutsy bastard. They'd sold more than seventy videotapes at twenty bucks a pop. The lad came up with some bellringers. But lately he'd gone off his bird. He was obsessed with that freak that lived out in the woods with her mama. He rode with the others in the van after school, but he wasn't there. Mostly he just read library books at the college, all about medical freaks. He loved those disgusting photographs.

"Fenton, you there? Pick up."

"Ey, Slick."

"You busy?"

"I got a date in a little while, so let's rap later. Bye, bye, m'man."

"Don't hang up," Casey said in a very easy voice. "You been avoiding me or what?"

"Hey, dingo, I'm just out of the shower and dripping all over the carpet."

"Cancel your date," Casey said.

"Who the hell are you talkin' to like that? Go sit on a sharp stick and do three-sixties till your hat flips."

"I've done a lot of stuff for you, Fen."

"Oh, yeah?"

"Yeah. Like accessing the school's computer bank and puffing up your abysmal grades?"

"So?"

"So I need you this afternoon . . . and this evening."

"Like I said, I'm busy. A previous engagement." Fenton toweled his chest and slung the towel over his shoulder. "What's your problem."

"Tit for tat," Casey said. "I'm calling a marker."

"You want some tit, try Gail."

"I don't want Gail. I want you to come to my house in half an hour and pick me up."

"Hey, you know, I don't care what you want." Fenton took a cigarette from a pack on his desk and lit up. "I taxi you around the whole damn county without charging you a penny, and I buy you dope, chicken wings, condoms."

"I can't drive," Casey said. "You know that."

"What's to convince me to run this little errand for you?"

"Friendship."

Fenton snorted. "Well, it's original anyway."

"Alright. How about a guarantee to zap ninety percent of all the reprimands on your permanent record, and I'll boost your gradepoint average another half a point so you can definitely get into your old man's alma mater."

This took Fenton by surprise. "You can do all that?"

"Yeah. I can do it."

"And you will, if I just drive you around tonight?

"Tonight's important to me."

"An interesting situation," Fenton said.

"Well?"

"I'll pick you up in forty minutes."

THE BOYS watched Muriel Nelson pedal her weird contraption straight through the stop sign that marked the intersection of Hull Rock Road and Pascal Lane. She was pointed in the direction of Sturgis.

"Like a clock," Roger Casey observed.

"She can really pump that thing. You'd think she was strad-dling a piston engine." Fenton squinted after the vanishing figure. "So where is it she goes every Monday, Wednesday and Friday?" Fenton Lindsey said.

"The dump mostly."

"The dump?"

"Yeah. Picks over stuff, looking for metal, engine parts, rags, clothes, whatever. Then she hauls it to the scrap metal dealer, the auto shop, and like that."

"She gets a late start," Fenton said.

"Dump doesn't close until six. She can't really sneak in until it's shut."

"They never catch her?"

Casey shrugged. "It's not exactly a gold mine. They look the other way, I suppose. She's been doing it for years."

"So," Fenton said. "Time for show and tell?"

"What do you mean?" Casey said.

"Give me some credit for minimal brain function, Slick. We're gonna party with your freak tonight, right?"

"Don't call her that," Casey said.

"Okay, okay. The Spook?"

"Her name's MaryAnn."

"How sophisticated." Fenton put the van in gear and gunned it out onto the gloomy tree-lined road. "What's the story, man? What does this little bitch do for you?"

Casey didn't answer.

"She's a mutation, right? Like maybe it's not just her face and brain pan that's all weirded up. You figure she's got something other girls don't have."

"Let's just get there," Casey said.

1 6 1

Fenton laughed. "Wouldn't miss it for the world. But how do we get past the ball-biting dogs. Or, hey, maybe if we wave some raw meat in the breeze, she'll smell it and gallop down to us. Think you could get a look while she was jumping and snapping with the other dogs?"

Casey didn't even smile. "Let me worry about the dogs."

"Sure." Fenton grinned. "Anything you say.

The mailbox hove into view around a turn and Fenton eased the van off the road opposite it. The gravel would leave no tracks to connect his van with this place. Turning off the engine, he slipped out and walked up to the gates a few paces behind Casey, who was carrying a paper bag. The day was overcast, as usual this time of year, and the light was going. Among the evergreens, it was already dark.

Fenton said, "I sure as hell don't feel like tangling with those four-legged furballs."

Casey didn't respond. He was staring at the dirt track leading up into the trees.

"We're here, Einstein. Now what?" Fenton said.

Casey sat on the ground and removed his black gloves from the bag.

"Whoa, man," Fenton said. "I get it."

The gun came out of the bag.

"We'll still have to hunt 'em down, though" Fenton said.

From the bottom of the bag, Casey took a dog whistle. He blew it three times, three long soundless blasts. The tops of the trees swayed in the wind. The forest made a whooshing sound and the sun shimmered through the topmost branches. And then they appeared, all four of them, bounding out of the darkening woods. In a minute they were rushing toward the fence, growling and raging, as if madness had been bred into them. They threw themselves against the barrier with fangs bared, barking and salivating.

"Four. That's all of them, isn't it?" Casey said, standing close to the fencing. The Dobermans and the shepherd leaped into the air, as if trying to vault it, or else lock onto some part of him that was higher up.

"That's all that showed last week," Fenton said.

"Right. Except that mangy stray."

"Who does the honors?"

"I will," Casey said, and popped off quiet shots that brought the four animals to the ground before they even realized they were under attack. Three more shots finished off the wounded.

Fenton beamed. "The target practice paid off, didn't it?" he said.

"Yeah," Casey said, "I'm murder up close."

"How come you wear gloves?"

"No fingerprints or gunpowder residue."

"Mine must be all over the piece from offing the cows."

"They are."

Casey reloaded as he stepped in front of the gate, then aimed at the lock and blew it to hell.

Fenton chuckled. "You think of everything."

"Hope so." Casey looked at his cohort. "Get the van while I swing these open."

Fenton Lindsey looked at the primitive driveway. He knew now, of course, that there could be major consequences from this outing. There was no way he was going to leave tire tracks all the way to the house and back. He squinted at Casey swinging open the gate.

"We walk," Fenton said.

Casey pushed the gate-half away. It jiggled as it pivoted. "No way," he said. "It will throw us off schedule. It'll be pitch black by the time we're done. We have to have the van close when we . . . ."

"Nobody's around," Fenton said, in a soothing voice. "It's a beautiful evening for a walk." And he strode through the gate and up the dirt track. "C'mon, Slick. Can't keep a girl waiting."

IN AMONG the trees the inky shadows were chilly. Somewhere behind the seasonal cloud cover, the sun was dropping quickly. The overcast tamped the stars and reduced the moon to a bluish blush in one corner of the sky.

From his knapsack, Casey took a flashlight with a single fat battery secured underneath, and he switched it on.

"Got another one?" Fenton asked.

"Nope. Just stay close when it gets really dark. You'll be okay."

"Only if insanity isn't catching."

They trekked up the rutted roadbed, dodging brush at the side of the road that threatened to reach across its width, ducking the odd tree limbs that jutted out at them like elbows.

"What do you think she'll look like?" Fenton said.

"How should I know?" Casey said, shrill with eagerness.

"You think she'll have two heads? I saw a kid in a supermarket mag who did. They had him in a bottle."

Ahead by a step, Casey shrugged his shoulders. "She could, I guess. Duo-cephalics are extremely rare, but not unknown."

He glanced back. "I doubt it, though. They hardly ever live past infancy, and they're usually considered two people. You know—two heads, two brains, two personalities. MaryAnn has always been spoken of as a single entity."

"Maybe she's got six tits, like a cat. Man, I'd pay to see that."

"We all have our dreams," Casey muttered. "All I'm sure of is that it's a major teratological problem."

"What the shit is that?"

"A really bad deformity."

"Oh."

"Like the Wolfgirl of Delphos, Kansas. That was a case in 1974. A similar thing: kid hidden from view since birth."

"Wow," Fenton said. "You can bet your ass it's something wild, though. The plastic surgeons now can retread almost anything. But not our darlin' MaryAnn." Fenton snickered. "My old man has had so much lifted all over 'im, he's six inches taller than he used to be."

For a while they fell silent, only their soles scraping along the roadbed.

"Maybe," Fenton said, "she's got too many arms and legs and looks like a giant white spider."

"Your imagination seems focused on multiplicity," Casey whispered. "Dramatic but unlikely. Isn't it more intriguing to picture her as an entirely new form of human life? Maybe she's the next step in our evolution and has mental and physical abilities that we can't conceive of now."

Fenton spat into the darkness. "That's science fiction bullshit."

"You're probably right."

"You bring a camera?"

"No," Casey said.

It was getting colder; damp, too. Casey's breath spewed, like a faint white cloud, into the shaft of light that led them.

"Why didn't you bring a camera?" Fenton said. "We could strip her, take a roll of shots and sell the prints for big-time money. Everybody would want a set."

"I'm not doing this for money. Or to make a public spectacle of her for every cretin in the state to get off on."

"Ey, Slick, it's just me and you out here. You can tell me. You want to get it on with her because she's a hermaphrodite, or to get her a meaningful job in a hoochie-coochie show?"

"Fuck off."

"This bitch really squeezes your 'nads, doesn't she?" Fenton laughed. "A case of true love. I never thought I'd see one. Oh, I read about a *case* out in Wisconsin, back in '82, but . . . ." Fenton cracked up at his own joke.

The derision had cut Roger Casey like a knife. There were ripostes he could have hurled back, but he held his tongue. Fenton was totally self-centered, privileged beyond all rational limits, yet unappreciative, smug, convinced his wealth and position insulated him permanently. It had distorted his personality. Fenton was heartless. Casey counted on that, played off it, used it. He also needed Fenton's size, weight, muscle. So he couldn't antagonize the proto-human.

"Fen, we may have some trouble with her."

"Hell, she won't be any problem for us, even if she can spin webs out of her butt. If she gives me any backtalk, ba-boom! She kisses the floor. If she's got lips, that is.

Fungus brain, Casey thought. "I mean, she may be a type of feral child. Like the Wolfgirl."

The boys were walking side by side now behind the beam of light. When Fenton looked at Casey with that off-center grin of his, only the whites of his eyes and the glitter of his teeth were visible.

"Feral, eh?" Fenton said. "I bet you don't think I know what that means."

"How could you not, what with a three point gradepoint average," Casey said, and chuckled to lessen the tension.

"There've been hundreds of them, right?" Fenton said. "All over India and places."

"Supposedly," Casey replied. "Ape children, sheep children, bear children, wolf children . . . . It's questionable, though, whether the stories have any valid bases. Some have been shown to be hoaxes, some involved retarded kids abandoned by their families. It's hard to know. The individuals have always been removed from their environments before impartial observers got a chance to verify the claims."

"You are crushing my comic book fantasies, Slick."

"The truth is hard," Casey sighed. "But I've seen film clips . . . there's this girl in the Spanish Sahara, right where there was supposed to have been a boy raised by gazelles about thirty years ago, and now she runs with them. She's gorgeous. Long black hair, white boobs. If she's a fake, they should pass a law to make her live that way."

"That's the way you imagine our MaryAnn, isn't it?"

"I don't know," Casey said faintly. "She could be just an impaired kid hidden away by kin. She may not even be able to speak."

"Another plus. The way I see it, mankind's troubles started when women were taught to talk."

"She might have the mental capacity of a baby. She might not wear clothing."

"Hey, hey, hey. This gets better as it goes along. You didn't happen to bring a diaper, did ya?"

Casey stopped walking and set his knapsack on the ground.

"What's the problem?" Fenton said. "Can't find the nappy?"

Casey felt around for the articles he had brought.

"C'mon, Slick. I don't want to spend the whole friggin' night out here."

The younger boy lay the articles on the ground in front of the light. "We'll need these to handle her."

"Yeah?" Fenton squatted. "Rubber cords? What's this, a sleeping bag?"

"These are to secure her wrists and ankles. This one, with the wedge attached, is to gag her. And the cloth bag is to keep her in while we drive back to my place."

"What? Are you nuts? What kind of kinky shit have you got in mind?"

"Fen— "

"You're going to screw this freak *and* take her home to meet the family. I'll be a son-of-a-bitch. Slick, my man, that's kidnapping, even if she isn't actually human."

"I can . . . I can make it better for her, Fen. There's this old house on my granddad's land, about two miles back of our place, and there's absolutely nothing near it: no other houses, no road. It's more isolated than this place. I can take her there. I can teach her, make a thinking human of her."

"You crazy bastard." Fenton grinned. "You want to own this little animal. Talk about perverted nooky." He slapped Roger Casey on the arm. "No way."

"But—"

"Ey, you want her? Have her. But packin' her off is a no-no."

"Fen."

"March, baby. We've got a ways to go yet."

They walked more than another mile before they topped a hill and Casey's light picked out the side of a half-ruined house.

Fenton made a face. "What a garbage pail. Do think this is where they live?"

"Must be. There doesn't seem to be any other place around."

"A honeymoon cottage for the bride of Dracula is what it looks like. If she's covered with running sores, you're on your own, bruddah."

"You said you'd help."

"I didn't say I'd risk infection."

"Defects aren't contagious," Casey said.

"She might have something else that is. She bares her teeth at me and it's the old hook-cross for your girlfriend. Or better yet—" Fenton reached into Roger Casey's open backpack and withdrew the handgun.

Casey pulled away but the gun remained in Fenton's hand. Casey said, "Give me the gun, man."

"I don't think so."

"Do it, Fenton. We didn't come here to hurt her."

"You only know why you came, ass bite. You want a little recreation? Great. Me, I have other interests."

"Leave," Casey said, cool, composed. "I'll take care of everything. Take your van. Go."

"Not this far in, bub."

1 6 9

Casey's hand knocked the gun away. It spun into the night just as the heavy flashlight connected with Fenton's head and dropped him onto his backside. Casey jabbed at him with both fists.

Stunned but hardly helpless, Fenton slipped into the pattern rehearsed by his synapses during countless hours of martial arts drills. He flipped Casey aside, as if he was a rowdy pet. The boy hit the ground hard, and the flashlight shot off in one direction, his glasses in another. He emitted a grunt and wheezed. Deprived of breath, he could only watch the shadow that was Fenton spring to his feet and approach. A vicious kick made a searing pain combust in Casey's side at the point of impact.

"Want more, dipshit?"

Casey was too desperately busy trying to breathe to answer. Fenton grasped his shirt and jerked him to his feet.

"Answer me, or I'll take it as a yes and we'll dance some more."

"No," Casey said, choking.

Fenton shoved him away contemptuously, and Roger Casey fell to the ground again. The older youth quickly found the gun and the flashlight and returned to Casey, who was frantically fumbling through the long grass.

"You wanted her," Fenton said, "so come on."

CASEY STAGGERED blindly ahead. With his hair wildly dishevelled, the backpack twisted crazily on his back, and his eyes squinty, trying to focus without glasses, he didn't look so formidable. But the voice had regained its former authority.

"If you kill her, Fenton, I'll report it to the police."

"In that case, maybe I'll leave two bodies up here. Move your ass, professor."

Casey stumbled toward the house.

In spite of the terrible condition of half of the structure, what was left was solidly repaired and tightly locked. The front door was at least two inches thick; the surviving windows were sealed off by crude but effective pine slat shutters mounted on the inside. It seemed the only way in was to kick in the door, or a set of shutters, which probably would give the freak a chance to escape to the woods . . . if she was inside at all.

"She's not even here," Casey said. "Let's go before her mother gets back."

"Shut up," Fenton said, and kicked the front door. "Hey! You in there. MaryAnn!"

"Who is it?" a voice said from close by in the house.

"She's there," Casey said. "She can speak."

"That don't necessarily mean she wears clothes," Fenton said quietly, then loudly shouted, "It's me, Cyrano, and your secret admirer, Captain Midnight. We're coming to you, baby. The boogeymen are here!"

"Go," said the voice. "Leave us alone, or I'll call the boys."

"Boys?" Fenton repeated. "You said the bitches live alone."

"Far as I know," Casey said.

"Call the boys, MaryAnn," Fenton shouted. "Bring 'em on, baby." He released the safety on the pistol and shone the light around the yard.

"Apollyon!" the voice called. "Malphas. Ahriman."

"What the hell names are those?" Fenton said.

"Jesus," Casey said, leaning back against the wall of the house. "They're demons and angels."

"You mean, she's calling spirits on us?"

"Lucifer!" the voice shouted. "Lu-ci-fer!"

"You don't have to tell me that one," Fenton said, and then he caught on. "The dogs." He almost laughed. "They're dead, darlin'," he yelled. "We popped 'em — bang, bang, bang. Open the door!"

"Benjees!"

Fenton looked to Casey, huddled against the wall. "Benjy?"

"Maybe she's got a brother."

"Yeah, growing out of her left cheek. Watch out." Fenton reared back and kicked the door hard, once, twice, grunting loudly with each blow. The door held as he continued kicking, though the house seemed to actually tremble.

"Go away," the voice begged.

Fenton kicked the door again, and stopped. His foot throbbed. "Damn. Open up, doll."

Casey sneered. "I thought you could karate your way through anything."

Fenton brought his arm up slowly, dramatically. His hand and the gun came level with Casey's face. "I told you once, I told you twice . . . ." His eyes followed the slant of the flashlight along the stone foundation and where it ran into the hillside. "Hey," he said, "your cherry days may be over yet."

Shoving Casey ahead of him, he made for the back of the house. A place this old would have a dirt basement and, on the downhill side, a door into it from the outside. And there it was.

"Bingo," Fenton said.

The door panel swung open—but back and up. It was hinged at the top. They must have kept dogs down here. There was probably an interior door, too, leading up into the house proper. He prodded Casey with the gun barrel.

"Go, Romeo."

Casey, hunched over, pushed his way inside, Fenton close behind him. The air was heavy with the smell of fur and dog food and excrement.

"Give me the flashlight," Casey said.

"I've got it, man. Don't wet your drawers. God, it smells in here."

"What did you expect?" Casey pivoted slowly, listening. "Shine it around and find the door so we can get back out of here."

Fenton swept the light around the surprisingly large room. Dirt floor, stone foundation, uncovered joists, flooring about four feet over their heads, spiderwebs, animal skulls, wooden steps . . . going up.

"There we are," Fenton said.

"Where?"

"Dead on, Eagle Eye." Fenton nudged him forward; Casey was sweating in spite of the cold night. The dirt floor rose higher as they neared the stairs. "Start crawling," Fenton ordered, "and watch out for low beams."

As Fenton played the light over Casey's shoulder to show the way, something soared into it, snarling. A hairy body. Dog! Fenton cursed and kicked; the beast growled, its jaws snapping. The flashlight fell away, its beam cupped and made tiny by the wall. The door Casey had feared a second earlier, now became the likeliest escape route and he clambered up the wooden steps on his hands and knees, grunting with fear and effort. Fenton was right with him, shouting and thrashing.

The door flew open. The girl stood before them, hoodless, a shock of white hair framing the black truth of her face. Fangs gleamed. She snarled like a mad dog. Something hard struck Roger Casey above the brow and knocked his head back into Fenton's. Agony rang through Casey's skull and the night went technicolor. He fell backwards, into the black cellar, colliding again with Fenton, who was spitting muffled curses and clutching his nose.

"Oh, Jesus," Fenton cried. "It's her!"

There was a hideous growl and Casey heard the muted phfffft of the silenced pistol.

"Get away!" Fenton screamed, and fired twice more. The last shot ricocheted off the stone wall with a clack. Fenton was hysterical. He screamed for help.

The noises of struggle were close to Roger Casey, so close that he could feel the vibrations on his face. Terrified, he leaped at the sound anyway, struck someone-something in the pitch black. Teeth raked his arm, the hot breath of the beast joined by the sudden heat of blood—his.

"Kill!" the voice screamed and fangs pierced his lower lip and ripped it into flaps. He felt the slashing damage more intensely than he would have imagined, so powerfully that his own screams almost deafened him.

He thrashed madly. The thing was massive, hairy. His ear ripped away and he yowled like an animal frantic to flee. He crawled and realized suddenly that his forearm was laid open to the bone, flesh dangling. Behind him Fenton Lindsey pleaded and wailed while the thing tore at him, and Roger

Casey competed with shrieks so loud that he was himself
amazed. Then his hand slapped the earthen floor and the gun.
The weapon leapt into his grasp. He turned it toward the
hideous sounds and pulled the trigger, again and again, want-
ing to destroy everything in that dark hole, until the gun
clicked empty.

Whining, he curled into a ball, his body shaking. He had
never dreamed she would be like this. "Oh, God!" He lay
quaking for several seconds. The attack was not resumed.
The cellar was still. He heard jaws chomping. Something
lurched through the darkness, wheezing. *Feeding?*

Roger Casey crawled, desperately testing the wall, looking
for the way out. A cold wash of air hit him as the door swung
open on its hinges, and he plunged out into the night.

Outside, he moaned with pain and sheer horror. He had to
get out of there. She might be after him at any moment.
Fenton was surely dead or damaged beyond repair. If he didn't
want to join him, he had to act now.

Casey scrambled through the darkness. He barely heard
the groan that wound its way from his chest the entire time.
He made his way back around the building by touch, then ran
in the direction of the road, falling twice, the second time
badly. Blood wet his torso and face and legs. He forced
himself not to think about his wounds, forced himself to
concentrate on the hump in the middle of the roadbed as he
stumbled away.

The overhanging bushes and limbs struck out at him all
along the route. Slipping and stumbling, he managed the two
miles to the ridge overlooking the road and the bodies of the
dogs. A hard lump rose on his cheek until the jaw hinge was

stiff. Breathless, he lurched down the incline to the open gate, then across the road to the van. He could lock the van, he thought. Signal with the horn and lights. As he approached it, he realized he couldn't wait for someone to come by and help him. She was there in the woods, she and her hellish hound.

He clambered into the driver's seat. Though he had never driven in his life, the basic mechanics were simple, and he knew where Fenton kept the spare key behind the mirror in the sun visor overhead. He found it easily, dropped it, found it in his lap, put it in the ignition and turned. The engine started. He pulled the knob for the headlights and the dash lights came on as well. With his nose pressed close to the gear indicator, he made out the little arrowhead pointed to the "D", shoved hard on the gas pedal and pushed the lever to the letter. The shrieking van spun from the shoulder onto the paving and shot down the road.

Casey wrestled the machine along the roadway. With his myopia and lack of skill, the center stripe seemed like a fluorescent worm on whose wriggling back he barely managed to stay. Yet he forced the van forward at faster speeds, all the while praying for someone to come, to take him to safety, to the hospital, the police.

The house appeared only after he had careened along the road for almost five miles. Actually, he saw the security light mounted on a pole next to it, rather than the house itself. There would be someone home, there had to be, he thought. He whipped the speeding van into the driveway. He mistook the turn and missed. The front wheels dropped into the ditch on the side of the driveway. Casey's stomach dropped, too, and the front bumper slammed into the opposite bank with such force that he was thrown over the top of the steering wheel. His head cracked against the windshield, shattering it, while the van continued its journey toward the house, tumbling, then rolling madly, the boy like a rag doll inside.

It came to a stop, upside down, when it collided with a car parked in the driveway. The driver lay still on what had been the ceiling a half second before, not really certain if he was alive or dead. Dust billowed everywhere.

Lights came on in the house, people flooded out. A man's voice roared: "Damn son-of-a-bitch drunk bastards! Call an ambulance, Leona. And call the police."

Roger Casey closed his eyes and smiled with what was left of his lips. Yes, call them all, he thought. Call them all.

9

MURIEL NELSON was within earshot of the Scoggins place and heard the vehicle screech off the road and smash into Cletus's one year old Chevrolet, heard Cletus yell at his wife to call for an ambulance and the police.

She recognized the van as she drew nearer. It belonged to one of those teenaged jerks who had faced her down at the gate. From the speed that they'd been going when they hit the ditch and somersaulted across the lawn, she intuited trouble for herself. She hoped all six of them were dead, as she swept by quietly, legs pumping.

She worked the pedals with great energy and the cold night air flowed into and out of her lungs like burning fluid. She propelled the cycle far beyond the accident scene and into the black funnel of Hull Rock Road, where the only light came from the clouded moon and the narrow lamp on her handlebars. In remarkably short time, she traveled the remaining five miles to her turnoff. When she saw the dogs alongside the open gate, she mumbled, "My babies," and wondered about the fate of her daughter. Without pausing, she pedaled onto the hard dirt track and up the hill. Two miles later, she arrived, breathless, in her yard. The front door, she saw, remained locked. Was MaryAnn running with the dogs out in the woods? Had she been sleeping amongst them again beneath the house and escaped through the back? Unclipping the cycle lamp, she shone it at the house. The circle of light grew smaller as she went to the door, unlocked it and stepped inside.

"MaryAnn."

"Some men came, Mama?"

Muriel raised the lantern. It shone on her hooded daughter. The sleeves and bodice of the dress were torn, as was the hem. Her arms and one exposed breast glistened with blood. The dress was darkly stained.

"Are you hurt?"

"No, Mama."

"What did they do?"

The girl was trembling all over. "They were going to hurt me. Mama? The boys didn't come when I whistled."

Muriel Nelson gulped a large breath. She lit a kerosene lamp on the table and looked again at her daughter. "How did they get in?"

"The cellar."

She saw the door to the basement stood open and went to the doorway. The cycle lamp shone on a sneaker jutting out from behind one of the long raw logs she had used to prop up the flooring. Calmly she descended the stairs and stooped over the bag of flesh. He would have been lying face up, she guessed. In addition to the missing features, his throat was rent from chin to sternum. She stood away. The body steamed in the biting cold, the vapors rising from it like a languid spirit abandoning its host. Against the far wall lay their oldest dog. Muriel ducked her head and climbed back upstairs. MaryAnn hadn't moved.

"What have you done?" Muriel said.

MaryAnn stood quiet.

"What have you done?"

MaryAnn stared. "I'm sorry, Mama," she whispered. "Really."

"What am I going to do?" Muriel said. There was a tremulous confusion in her tone that her daughter had never heard before. "Think," Muriel said to herself. "Think."

"Mama."

"Shut up!"

"Yes, Mama."

"Let me think."

Muriel busied herself with small inane chores: pumping herself a cup of water at the sink, rinsing the glass, lighting another kerosene lamp. What was she to do? But, of course, she had known for a long time.

"The one in the cellar is dead, isn't he?" MaryAnn said.

"Pretty much," Muriel replied, absently.

"Why don't you put him where you put the other two, and nobody will know."

"What?"

"The man who ran was too scared to come back."

Muriel held a hand to her eyes. "There weren't any 'two'," she said, and suddenly took her daughter's wrist. "Not any. Never. You understand?"

"Yes, Mama."

"Nobody, ever." Muriel pushed the wrist away roughly. "Go to your bed," she snapped.

MaryAnn slid away to her room. Bed springs creaked. Muriel went to the cutlery drawer. The knife she chose was long and glistening. Finely tempered steel. She slipped it behind her belt in back and covered it with her shirt. The shaft was cold against her buttock.

MaryAnn was sitting on the bed when Muriel entered. She went to the child and extended a hand to touch her shoulder. MaryAnn, expecting a blow, drew away. Muriel put her hand gently on her daughter's shoulder and MaryAnn allowed herself to rest her cloaked head against her mother's arm. She did not lean against it, however, as she knew Mama didn't like to touch.

"MaryAnn, there are people coming back here tonight."

"More men?"

"Yes. The police, too."

"Oh, Mama." Her breath caught. "I don't want them here."

"There's nothing we can do, darling."

Darling. Mama had hardly ever called her that, not for years and years.

"Will they hurt us?" MaryAnn said.

Muriel said nothing.

"What can we do?"

"Stand up."

MaryAnn stood dutifully and held the flap of her torn dress against her bosom with a bloody hand.

"Turn around."

MaryAnn pivoted slowly, trembling. "They'll cut my face and make me go without my hood so people will laugh. And they'll take you away from me." Her voice shook. "Can we run away?"

Muriel positioned the girl from behind. "We can't run faster than cars."

"Maybe you can make them not come."

"Shh. Don't talk," she said. It was better not to draw it out. "Remember the puppy you had two years ago, the one you found in the sack by the road? What did you call it?"

"Thursday," MaryAnn whispered. "I found her on Thursday, so I called her that."

"She was pretty, wasn't she? With that white spot behind her eye."

"She was so *fat,*" MaryAnn cackled. "She rolled around like a ball when I petted her. And one night . . . that night when she was crying all the time—when we first got her—I had to put her in my bed the whole time, and she thought *I* was her mom."

Quick, Muriel thought. I can do this.

"And then Benjees killed her," MaryAnn said. She suddenly looked back. "Why did he eat her, Mama?"

"It just happens sometimes. Death is part of life."

The girl turned away again. "Now Benjees is dead, too. Yes, Mama?"

"Yes."

"He was very fierce. He was the only dog who slept apart from the rest of us," she said, then fell silent, remembering that she wasn't supposed to bed down with the dogs in the cellar, although she had since she'd been six.

Muriel eased the knife from her belt and interlaced her fingers around the handle, holding it blade down.

"He never ran with us."

Muriel took the knife in both hands and raised it above her head, just as a siren wafted across the night sky.

The girl turned and her eyes widened at the sight of her mother holding the knife. "Mama."

"Shush." She lowered the knife.

"Is it them?"

"Probably," Muriel said, sounding resigned. She pushed the knife back under her belt.

"Please don't let them take me and hurt me. I won't ever be terrible again. I solemnly swear. Mama . . . ." She slipped to her knees and began rocking. "Please."

Muriel rushed to the front door. She couldn't see their lights yet, but the wail of the approaching siren was growing louder. "Goddamn you," she said, and slammed the door hard against its frame. It banged shut and popped open again from the force. A globe of light moved through the woods. Muriel went back to the girl's room.

"Get up," she said.

"I don't want them here, Mama." The girl wailed. "Make them go."

Muriel pulled MaryAnn to her feet. "You've got to go from here. Run into the woods."

"Yes!" MaryAnn grasped her mother's hands. "We can run."

"No. I have to stay and explain." The siren was closer. "You go through the dog pen and run as fast as you can."

"Come, too, Mama. I don't want them to hurt you."

"They won't. Now, go. Go toward the caves if you have to, and if they bring more people, cross the road into the next woods. Don't go near any houses and don't let them catch you."

"Can't I come back? When can I come back?"

"When no one is chasing you anymore." Muriel pulled a plastic sling bag from the peg and the sweater next to it, shoved it inside, next to the skinning knife, and looped the drawstring over her daughter's head and shoulder. "I'll tell them what happened and I think they'll believe me. And then you can come back . . . when they're gone. Now, go."

The girl clutched at her. "I'm scared, Mama. Please come with me!"

Muriel punched her arm. "Get the hell out of here!" she hissed.

Whimpering, MaryAnn ran to the far corner of her room and lifted the planks up from the floor in a practiced motion, then, with amazing agility, dropped to the earthen basement below.

OFFICER PHILLIPS held onto the dashboard and the door as the patrol car rocked along the crude dirt road toward the Nelson place.

"God," he said, "what a night."

James Lowell never took his eyes off the road and the rocks and saplings embedded in it. The car clunked the rocks and the baby trees whooshed along the undercarriage.

"We don't know what we've got," he said, "other than a

stoned shithead who's cracked up a vehicle and probably addled his brains in the wreck."

"You heard what he was babbling. His sidekick torn up and dead, that monster kid on the loose."

The flashing blue lights atop the roof scythed the forest. Lowell wrestled the wheel, letting the ruts lead him, forcing the car to one side or the other to avoid whatever he could. A pine branch caught the top of the car and bent back with its force, then slipped off and scraped along the roof.

"Jeeze," Phillips said. "Ivan Lindsey's boy."

"Don't jump to conclusions," Lowell said and grunted as he pulled the wheel hard, away from an oncoming rock that stuck out like a gopher. The front tire hit it anyway and the car bounced over it.

"I mean, everybody knows she's a dangerous freak. Crazier than a junkyard dog. Fuckin' evil. I grew up on Washington Road. There have been stories about her around here for years. They say—"

"'They say.' They say there are werewolves living in secret military installations in California."

"This kid ain't even human. People disappear around her. Did you see how chewed up that kid was."

"The kid asked for it."

Suddenly they topped a hill and the house sprang into the headlights.

"Christ," Phillips muttered, as Lowell skidded to a stop twenty feet from the door of the house, and cut the siren. The roof lights pivoted madly, spraying the house and woods with fractions of light.

"I see lights inside," Lowell said.

"How do you want to handle this?" Phillips pulled a shotgun from the rack in between them."

"You make the pitch while I cover the door from my side."

"Okay," Phillips said. "Anybody comes out and I'll shell their butts."

"Go easy with the howitzer."

"You know it. I'd rather be a moving target than a sitting duck," Phillips said, and whipped open his door, the microphone wire coiling after him like a spring.

Lowell stepped out slowly and drew his sidearm. Phillips leveled the shotgun at the doorway from behind the open car door and keyed the mike. Lowell slipped easily to the side of the house and flattened against the wall. The headlights' glare made him invisible to anyone inside.

"This is Officer Phillips, Duncan County Sheriff's Department. You are ordered to come out, hands on your head. Now, people."

The amplified announcement echoed through the woods and dissipated, leaving only the rustle of the wind in the treetops. Lowell trained his pistol on the empty doorway and eased his flashlight out of its belt holster.

"All right, all right!" a woman's voice yelled, and she stepped out, lantern in hand.

Lowell didn't see it, but Phillips did—the reflection from metal.

"Gun!" Phillips yelled. The shotgun belched pellets and Muriel Nelson's torso sprouted tiny geysers, as if in a cartoon, as her body jackknifed. Her arms shot out, her face to her knees, and she flopped right back into the house like a Jack-in-the-Box.

ROSS WALKER told Lola there was a form of communication that easily transcended broadcasting, and it went into operation whenever a major police emergency occurred. The rubber necker's telepathy party line, he called it, and Lola was forced to agree with him when they reached Hull Rock Road. The road was a barely moving caravan.

"All of these people," she exclaimed. "Where did they all come from?"

"North, east, south, west," Ross grumbled as he edged the car onto the shoulder. But several other drivers had had the same idea and were slowly inching forward in front of him. The flashing red light he had propped on the center of the dash didn't help at all. Every tow truck and farmer with jellybean lights atop his rig had them on and flashing. They were a good half mile from the turnoff to the Nelson place and creeping along.

"Incredible," she said.

"Don't tell me you never saw anything like this back home."

"In New York, one murder wouldn't even budge a seasoned citizen from his television, even if it was his next-door neighbor. This is unbelievable," she said.

"It's a big one," he said. "That boy's daddy is a prominent man."

What surprised her wasn't so much the presence of men and teenaged boys; she chalked this up to hormonal indoctrination. But the women and children . . . there were as many of them as of the men and boys.

"How did the news get around so fast?" she said.

"A few folks have police-band scanners on their CB radios, and everybody has a telephone."

A hard bump jolted the car. Lola grasped the windowframe. "And the guns?" she said.

Rifles, shotguns, pistols. They were mostly in the hands of men along the road, but sported by some of the women, too.

"This is a mob," she said, flatly. "An armed mob."

"They know a killer is loose . . . and Ivan Lindsey is well-known. They'll do everything they can to apprehend the killer of his son. That's how it works here."

"She'll never reach the station." Citizens' band radios hissed static at them as they passed the line of vehicles. "This is an execution squad. Some trigger-happy goof will accidentally dr—"

"Stop," he said. "She killed somebody. These people won't get past the mailbox. They'll gawk for a while and go home. The civil servants will find her and bring her in. That's our job. MaryAnn has rights."

"The same as the civil rights workers had? The same as the blacks, or anyone who's not a white Anglo?

"Hell, this isn't some Hollywood B movie from thirty years ago. Half the mayors in the state are black, and a black man is running for the statehouse. We're out here to apprehend a fleeing suspect. The law decides the rest. We're trained professionals, and this is still part of the United States, no matter how alien we all may seem to you." He pointed to uniformed lawmen along the side of the road. "They won't allow any civilians in here."

"How's the other boy?"

"Critical but stable."

"And Muriel Nelson?"

"The paramedics didn't think she was going to make it."

It took twelve minutes to reach the Nelson turnoff. Ross swung his car out of the procession of gawkers and stopped at the fence. Two marked cars blocked the entrance. Another ten were parked just beyond. There must have been police cruisers from all the surrounding counties, and several even from across the Tennessee line.

A sheriff's deputy strode toward them, shouting. "Hey. Hey, you. Keep moving. Get that junk heap out of here."

Ross slid out of the car, one foot on the ground, the other propped on the floorboard.

"Oh, Ross-man," the deputy said without embarrassment. "Didn't recognize you."

"What's the score, Matt?"

"The Lindsey kid got ground up by a mental case." He almost sounded joyous with excitement. "And that damn-fool Guy Phillips laid out the suspect's mama with a shotgun."

"She gonna make it?"

Matt shook his head. "Died. 'Bout an hour ago. Guy's in a pack of trouble."

"So much for restraint," Lola muttered, loud enough for Ross to hear but not the other deputy.

"Any sign of the suspect?" Ross said.

"Not yet. Malone thinks she's still on the property and we've got men on the perimeter. The lot runs two miles back into the hills. There's no road to the northwest, though. Just woods. If she goes that way, there's nothing between here and Memphis but woods. And the kid who did him is pretty amazing, I hear. Built like a goddamned monkey. They say she could probably shinny up an icicle."

"You been listening to wild stories, Matt?" Ross said.

Matt arched his eyebrows. "Maybe not so wild. I saw the Lindsey boy. He's still up there." He jabbed a thumb in the direction of the house. "It's like somebody shoved him through a pulp shredder. The kid looks filleted. Never saw nothin' like it." Matt noticed the passenger. "Ma'am," he said to her in greeting, then to Ross, "We're not supposed to let any civilians in."

"She's a public official herself," he said, "and she's been investigating the family situation."

"Okay," Matt said, and politely stepped back, waving them through and looking past them to the next vehicle pulling in.

THERE WAS a Cadillac to one side, an ambulance, a private car, and three patrol wagons with engines running and headlights trained on the house, forming an aurora amongst the trees atop the hill on which the Nelson house sat. Ross pulled in behind them and he and Lola got out.

"Howdy," James Lowell said. Another deputy stood beside him, nervously smoking, looking unhappy.

"Any sign of her?" Lola asked.

"Nope," Lowell replied.

"Damn," said the other deputy. "I wish the sheriff would let us get out there and find the bitch. This perimeter shit is getting us nowhere. At this rate, she could gnaw down half the community by sunup."

"Ease off, Guy," Ross said, and introduced Lola to Deputy Phillips, who nodded and moved on quickly, pacing around the house, eyes scanning the woods beyond.

"He's a little wired up," Lowell said.

Lola made no effort to hide her opinion. "Guy Phillips of the search and destroy division," she said.

"We'll find her," Ross said, and wondered if Malone wasn't going to send Phillips home, pending an inquiry.

"Malone's in the house," Lowell said, "but it's mighty crowded in there right now. Besides . . . ."

"Yeah," Ross nodded. "We'll wait out here."

"Who's that?" Lola said, looking at the Cadillac.

"The boy's daddy," Lowell replied in a low voice.

"C'mon," Ross said, and led them over.

Deputy Sheriff Martha Guntzelman was standing next to him, notebook open. Ivan Lindsey half sat on the hood of his spotless car and wept. His only child was dead. The boy he had once found a nuisance, he now mourned with all his heart.

"Are you sure there's no way to get in touch with your wife, Mr. Lindsey?" Martha asked.

"I don't think so," he said. "She's enroute to Barbados. I've called ahead and left urgent messages for her."

The crime scene photographer exited the house, carting his portable lights. He was followed by a deputy and the emergency room doctor who had ridden out in the ambulance.

"Maybe you should go home," Martha Guntzelman was saying to Ivan Lindsey.

"Not while my boy's still here," he said.

Through the door came Sheriff Malone holding his portable radio, and the ambulance attendants carrying a stretcher with the body securely strapped on. It was entirely draped in a metallic emergency blanket intended for preserving the body temperature of shock victims.

Ivan Lindsey turned away and bowed across the hood of the Cadillac. "Oh, God."

Malone motioned the attendants to hurry and pushed back the brim of his cap. Everything was silent for a moment, even, oddly, all the police radios. Ivan Lindsey suddenly stood away from his automobile and straightened to his full height. He turned to his son's body being borne past, then spun to face the dark forest.

"You crazy bitch!"

Martha Guntzelman moved to comfort him.

"Come out and show your face, you goddamned freak!" he screamed, and broke down, sobbing. The birds burst into song.

"Get him home," Sheriff Malone ordered, and Deputy Guntzelman led him off to a police car. The ambulance started off, slowly bouncing along the dirt road. The police car followed. The sky was growing lighter.

"You must be Dr. Aragon," Sheriff Malone said in his best paternal voice, and introduced himself while his officers stood around them in a loose circle, one of them monitoring the portable radio. "Tell me," the sheriff said, "what are we dealing with here? We need someone who's familiar with this MaryAnn Nelson. What can you tell us?"

"I never actually met her," Lola said.

"Is her brain affected by the deformities? Can she think at all? Can we reason with her somehow?"

"She's not an animal. She can speak. She talked to us quite reasonably. But you're asking if she's mentally defective. I . . . ."

"The young doc who rode in with the ambulance said it would be a wonder if she wasn't mentally deficient with so severe a physical problem."

Lola's tempered flared. "That's irresponsible of him, and medically unethical. He doesn't know anything about her firsthand."

"He knew he just signed a death certificate for an eighteen year old with his throat torn out." Malone rubbed his chin. "Is there anybody who's had dealings with her, or who could provide information? A welfare investigator? Social worker?"

Lola shook her head. "Only maybe Dr. Endicott. That's who briefed us, but he doesn't really know her either."

"I'll take what I can get," Malone said. He sighed. "We'll give him a call." He nodded to the deputy with the radio and the man turned away to enunciate the Sheriff's request for a landline-patch call to Dr. Endicott.

"Someday," said Malone, "we'll get them cellular phones."

"Sheriff," Lola said, "don't you think this operation is bordering on the ludicrous? You've got dozens and dozens of people down there on the road, and police all over, all looking for a teenaged girl who was probably just defending herself from attack."

Malone gave a condescending smile. "It's getting more complicated by the minute, Miss."

"Meaning?"

"The coroner left with the body of Mrs. Nelson, before you

two arrived. It's not conclusive, but he's making noises about similarities in the marks on the Jane and John Doe victims that surfaced at the dump a while back and some of those on the Lindsey boy."

"Oh, no," Lola said.

"So this is kind of expanding on us. The switchboard back in town is taking calls from news organizations all over the country. By midday the place will be a three ring circus . . . if we don't find her quick."

"And even if we do," Ross said, blowing on his hands.

Malone nodded. "You're probably right."

"You think MaryAnn hacked those two people to pieces?" Lola said.

"We just arrest 'em," Malone said. "We don't convict 'em. I'd just like to locate and detain the little lady without anymore bloodshed." He touched his hat. "Well, I've got to check on the coroner and notify the state police," he said and trudged off toward one of the police cruisers.

"Folks," Lowell said. "You might want to look inside. Found this in there, by the way." He held up a clear plastic bag with a finely tooled black axe inside it. "Climber's hatchet," he said. "This one's sharp as a Japanese sword."

Ross and Lola looked at him, then at one another.

"Okay," Ross said, and led Lola to the boarded up house and in through the one working door.

Inside, the place was a shambles. The floor they walked across was sticky but neither of them mentioned the slight viscous pull on their soles.

It was a little hard to see, but the sun was coming up fast. The first room—the kitchen-dining room with the fireplace and Muriel's cot—was pretty much the hodge-podge they remembered.

"In there," Lowell said, standing in the doorway and pointing to the girl's room.

Lola and Ross pushed open the door and went in.

The room was illuminated by two kerosene lamps sitting on the lone table. There was a bed and the table and the lamps—the only furnishings. But the spaciousness of the room was startling. It must have once been the parlor, an elegant room, with a high vaulted ceiling. The plaster was gone from the outside wall, leaving the latheing exposed. It was evident all the walls had been patched many times, and that the room had endured several injurious storms and at least one fire. Things were stuck into the nooks and crannies of the exposed lathes, and there were rows and rows of containers lined up along the baseboards.

Lola knelt beneath the boarded up window, Ross beside her with a lamp. Together they examined the countless jars filled with seeds, stalks of dried weeds stripped down to their fibers, aquatic egg sacs suspended in filmy water, birds' nests, berries, moss, tar, charcoal, balls of various furs, sticks, threads, bottles of colored liquid. Small wooden figurines peered out of crude niches running all the way up, teeth, eyeglasses, stones, the skin of a fish, the hide of a rattlesnake, felt tipped pens, mummified birds, lizards, frogs, beetles, rodents, a bottle of drowsy fireflies. Ross identified the contents as he went along.

"Red alder leaves, wild peppermint, resin, penny royal leaves, dewberry root, ashes, an old wasps' nest, slaked lime, chestnuts, catnip, rattlesnake weed . . . ."

A corner was filled with bowls of various sizes and shapes, each draped with a red stained cloth. Ross lifted one, then another.

"What's there?" she said, swallowing.

"Clay. Red Georgia clay . . . mixed with something else."

"Look," she said, pointing at the next wall.

It was covered with huge schematics of whole skeletons and partial bone structures: portions of a raccoon's skull, a cow's, a deer's, a fox's entire skeletal structure, a snake's skull and fangs, a whole rabbit in boney profile, and then a series of unintelligible profiles that combined the features from the various species to form fantasic, awesome new ones.

The last wall was filled with round faces devoid of features, other than haunting, empty eyes and vague Os for mouths. They were the same forbidding heads she had seen in the bas relief on Dr. Endicott's wall, the work of MaryAnn Nelson, fugitive, victim, unknown artist with an unknowable future. Whatever malformation Muriel Nelson had passed unwittingly to her daughter, she had also bequeathed her talent. Perhaps a great talent—primitive, eerie, savage.

The light in the room had gradually changed, Lola noticed. But how? The windows were boarded over. She stepped back from the wall, bumping into the bed. The sheets were a strange blue and becoming bluer, then black, then—. The room was changing color.

She looked up. It was as if the light had ignited the ceiling. Myriad bottles, pushed through crude chinking, caught the light and sent it down through the tapestry of glass. Glass disks . . . everywhere, in the most complicated arrays. They dotted the vaulted roof and had washed the room with the blue that was now turning reddish. The figures on the walls, the mummified creatures, everything shone brightly, and gave them the illusion of movement as the cerulean hues yielded to the coursing magenta.

The clay in the bowls turned a deep red, as did the ceiling, walls, floor, her skin. In moments the mood had changed. Lola looked to Ross. He stood, iridescent, and gaped at the ceiling, his skin and clothes crimson and speckled, as if drenched in blood.

10

DR. ENDICOTT looked older to Lola Aragon. Perhaps it was the sailcloth slacks, stained green at the knees where he had knelt in the garden that afternoon. Or maybe the slightly mussed aspect of his otherwise perfectly-parted patrician white locks. He was still wearing his deerskin gardening gloves and removed them now before he offered his hand.

"Dr. Aragon. What a surprise. Come in, come in."

He chatted amiably as he led her through the large, cool foyer and into the long hall that led to the house proper, past the formal dining room, billiards room, sitting room, library, the west art room, the east art room, the wing that housed the many portraits of his blue-eyed and finely-boned blond ancestors and family, through a sunny hall, and out onto a luxurious patio, shaded with trellised climbing roses, each perfectly yellow, perfectly formed.

Tea was already set out on the glass-topped table, with

extra cups, as always. Dr. Endicott ushered her to a rattan chair, older than she, and did the honors. He said he took his tea with milk, no sugar; she said she took hers "plain". He served her with the cozy flourish of one practiced in drawing room niceties, a man comfortable with people of all stations in life, a Southern gentleman with the common touch so invaluable to the medical practitioner. Too bad he had lost interest in it, Lola thought.

"I take it," she said, "that you've spoken with the sheriff."

He nodded, balancing the saucer in one hand, holding the cup by its graceful handle with the other, the translucent side revealing the dark shadow of the tea. The sun was strong but the wind nipped at her skirt and chilled her skin.

"Sheriff Malone interviewed me at length, by telephone. I heard the rest on the radio," he said.

"The second boy is in guarded condition, but when he's conscious he is pretty emphatic that MaryAnn Nelson and one of the dogs attacked Ivan Lindsey's son, and him, too . . . that she ordered it."

"I know Ivan Lindsey and his wife. I can hardly believe they've lost their boy."

"May I ask you what you told the police?" she asked.

"I can't see why not. It's pretty much what I told you and Deputy Walker that day you called on me. The sheriff, however, seemed to have his own agenda and pressed me quite hard."

"In what way?"

"He wanted to know if the girl was capable of killing with her hands and teeth. I objected to the question and said I couldn't give him a definitive answer without examining her.

No one could. Whereupon he chose to conclude that I could not definitively refute the possibility."

Lola sat back; the doctor's account of his conversation weighed on her. She half wished she hadn't asked.

"I explained to him—or tried to—that, medically speaking, 'monster' was an inappropriate term to employ. He became fairly shirty and said to spare him the thirty syllable explanation."

"Sounds like he had a long night."

"Yes," Dr. Endicott agreed. "Mind you, I don't think this monster business will hold up legally, but there is a real danger to her in the interim, if this is the attitude with which they attempt to apprehend her."

"I thought so, too, last night," she said. "When I suggested that MaryAnn might be frightened of men, having been raised exclusively by a woman, and urged them to have female volunteers walk the property with bullhorns, the sheriff told me he had lady officers, thank you very much, and that I should not trouble myself further."

"Well," said Endicott, "perhaps he'll act on your advice."

"Perhaps," she said.

He sipped his tea, and said, "Are you very worried about her safety?"

"Yes."

He nodded slowly.

She said, "I would like to ask you something, doctor."

"Certainly."

"It's somewhat personal."

"If you wish confidentiality, I can assure you I can be discreet."

"I don't doubt it." She put her beautiful cup down on the glass of the veranda table they shared. "There was more of MaryAnn's art out at her home—in her rather amazing room, and in the barn. She evidently gathered clays, made crude brushes, gouging tools, chisels, and collected materials of an infinite variety. You have to see it to understand. There is such talent there. I have to believe there is intelligence as well."

"There might well be. But there doesn't have to be."

"You said, I believe, that in instances of such severe deformity, it's rare for an infant to survive very long, much less reach childhood . . . puberty."

"Indeed. Since the organism is physiologically so compromised, it's extremely unusual for her . . . ." Dr. Endicott's attention was riveted on some thought.

"To have lived?" Lola said, prompting him.

"Mmmm. Yes."

"You had such an odd look just now, doctor."

"Oh, sorry. I was momentarily distracted."

"Were you thinking of Muriel Nelson?"

Dr. Endicott looked directly at her. "Are you sure there isn't any gypsy blood in your Mexican lineage?" He smiled faintly. "Yes, I was thinking of Muriel Nelson."

"Doctor . . . ." It seemed difficult for Lola Aragon to continue.

"Yes, my dear."

"I feel responsible for her child's survival now."

"You shouldn't take it upon yourself, really. Your intentions were the best."

"That's immaterial. It's how I feel. I want to help her, if I can."

"Yes."

"But I need you to help me first."

Dr. Endicott sipped his tea. "How?" he said.

"Tell me about the night MaryAnn was born."

"Yes . . . well, as I've recounted to you, I wasn't myself present at the birth. Her mother delivered the child herself. Even cut the umbilical cord."

"A formidable woman."

"Very."

"Did she love the child?"

"Oh, yes. I . . . I'm sure. Perhaps even too much."

"She was a strong-willed, domineering personality."

"Yes," he said, "but tempered by her confidence in her talent and its inevitable recognition."

"Except the recognition didn't come."

"No." He made a helpless gesture. "She had a real flair. Something was there, on the verge of coming forth. It just didn't happen. She was stylistically out of sync with the art trends, most certainly, but her talent could have overcome that eventually, if she hadn't been so frustrated by her initial neglect."

Lola glanced at the yellow climbing roses, moving ever so slightly in the chill breeze, and at the lush green perfection of the lawn.

"I'm truly sorry about this situation," Endicott said.

"I know."

"I never meant for this to happen."

"You couldn't have foreseen it, doctor." She looked back to him. "Even if you do feel particularly responsible."

"I don't feel *un*responsible," he said.

"You mean because you fathered her child?"

A cloud passed over, darkening the lawn as it lumbered by. He looked away. The surface of the tea in his cup was perfectly still.

"You're in the wrong line of work, Dr. Aragon."

"This is between us," she said. "I have my professional confidences, too. This will remain one of them."

She waited. He said nothing.

With an air of annoyance, he finally said, "May I ask how you came by this particular conjecture."

"I had a friendly New York banker tap into your local bank account for a friendly credit check."

"And you found black mail payments?"

"No."

"Financial scandal?"

"No."

"No, I shouldn't think so," he said coolly. "What then, Dr. Aragon? What prompted this leap of the imagination?"

"Your attempts to pay Muriel Nelson's land taxes for several years running. About eight in a row."

He colored slightly. "Is this a purposeful pursuit?" he said.

"I believe so."

Dr. Endicott sat silent.

"Doctor?"

He put aside the cup. Then, after a moment's thought, he said, "Yes. I . . . I sat for Muriel. We talked. Perhaps we fell in love . . . for a time. No, that's not quite true. I felt from the very first that she was attracted. And I was drawn to her as well. It was a difficult period insofar as my own marriage. I thought she was a bohemian, a worldly artist dedicated to her career, ruled by ambition, as I was. I imagined having a wonderful, rapturous totally free affair. In fact, we did."

"You wanted no threat to your well ordered life, however."

"No. I hadn't . . . I didn't anticipate her claiming me, pressing me to run off, divorce." He touched his hair. "I couldn't, of course. It was unthinkable. I was much older, married for thirty years, in politics. It would look silly, be silly. I told her this. She laughed and said it was too bad, because she was pregnant, with our child."

"Did you love her."

"I fantasized her and fell in love with the fantasy. You have no idea how boring a preordained existence can be, no matter how privileged. She was volatile, imaginative, wanton. But as her own ambitions grew more difficult to sustain, I realized she was also mercurial, possessive and increasingly desirous of finding a substitute for her career."

"Maybe she was in love with you."

"I'm honestly not sure. In any case, such a marriage would have been ruinous for both of us. The combination of her self-deception and my self-delusion was not a promising basis. I don't think she would have been happy with me as I truly was. And I think, eventually, she would have blamed me for the loss of her career. She couldn't see that. I had drawn her out, tantalized her with the implicit possibility of our staying together. I hadn't meant to, but I did . . . without question."

"And she had your child."

"Yes, she had MaryAnn." He smiled a wistful smile. "She named her for my mother. She was not without humor, black though it was."

"What happened when she was born?"

"Muriel would accept no medical care, no help, no support. She resisted and resented everyone who tried to aid her. I went out there to see if Muriel might listen to reason, and to pressure her as hard as I could to let me raise our baby and provide the child with the sort of opportunities Muriel couldn't. It would free her to pursue her painting, to try again for what she so needed. I offered financial assistance, entrée to art circles in Dallas and New York . . . . It was a selfish scheme, I suppose. I mostly just wanted my child, but there you are."

"How did Muriel Nelson respond to your proposal."

Joseph Endicott draped his elbow over the back of the rattan chair. "She said, 'Sure. Your wife will never suspect. Go ahead. Your baby's there . . . waiting for you.'"

ALL OF the day-glo "crime scene" ribbons had been ripped down. A quilted-aluminum food truck stood by the fence, servicing a lone deputy. The gates stood open and the track leading up to the Nelson place was deserted when Ross Walker turned off and followed the now familiar roadbed the two miles to the house.

A cruiser sat idle by the front door, face out, its driver slumped in the front seat, one foot on the dashboard, next to the microphone and a geological survey map of the Duncan County quadrant. Ross pulled in nose-first, between the brown and gold patrol car and the TV van with the dish antenna on top. From the center of the concave oval rose a pistil-like rod with a ball on the end. With their feet dangling out, a technician and a reporter sat in the open back. The techie was eating, the reporter was listening to himself on his cassette recorder.

"Mornin' Matt," Ross said.

Matt smiled. He looked tired and bored. "Howdy, pilgrim."

Ross slid out, careful not to bang his neighbor's car door with his own, and leaned down into the driver's side window.

The bright air was very still. No wind. Even the police radio was barely active. The reporter's smooth intonations were as lulling as the warm sun.

"I see the ranks of the media have thinned out some," Ross said.

Matt scoffed. "Hardly. They're in town, camped out opposite the city jail. There's radio and television crews from Dalton, Calhoun, Rome, Atlanta. And here's two from out of state: one from Chattanooga and one from Huntsville. The networks carried it last night on the evening news and Deborah Norville updated it this mornin' on *Today*. She gave 'em the down home, local girl's recollections of the region she come from." Matt yawned and reached for a thermos on the floor. "Some *pro*-ducers showed up just after you went off duty. They're talkin' good stuff 'bout wild-assed horror, tragedy, mini-series, made-for-TV movies. Duncan County's jumpin'" He poured himself some black coffee in the plastic cup that served also as the bottle's top and passed it over to Ross.

"You look mighty thrilled," Ross said, accepting the cup.

"I'm bushed," Matt said. "This is takin' a mite too long."

Ross took a sip and handed the coffee back. "Yeah. I take it the containment scheme hasn't worked."

"Nope. She's undoubtedly over the road, if not the state line. We're chasin' a devil. They've found no trace so far."

The reporter's taped voice weighed the possibility of new victims appearing in the girl's wake

Matt said, "What with all the stories, even our people are edgy. Everybody who can load a gun will be shootin' at her before long."

A small, light plane roared by overhead, skimming the pines.

"Searchers?" Ross said.

"Hardly. We've got helicopters up, but nothing fixed-wing."

The two officers followed the sound with their eyes, as if they could still see the aircraft.

Matt said, "It's flying low to avoid radar."

"You think it is what I think it is?"

"Yep," Matt said. "There must be four thousand private air strips in the state." He shook his head in resignation. "The new moonshine." He straightened and replaced the thermos top. "Hey, fella. Can you cover the frequency while I roll down to the roach wagon by the turnoff and replenish my java supply?"

"No problem," Ross said. "They're pickin' me up at the staging area down the road. I've got some time."

Matt keyed his mike and took himself out of service, and Ross slid in and announced himself on. A Dalton City cruiser pulled into the yard as Matt drove past. The Dalton City car parked next to Ross's—extra men sent over to help out. They got out and stretched; they were early for the next shift.

"I'm tellin' you," one sheriff's deputy said to the other, "she's got a head as big as a basketball, and long fungusy flaps hanging off and drippin' slime."

"You know this for a fact?" the other said.

More cars were bouncing along the dirt road toward the Nelson place. Unit 4 asked to stay on duty and join the next shift. Sheriff Malone came on the air. "No way, son," he said, sounding appreciative. "That's not good on a man. Go home, take six or seven hours, get some food in your belly and some rest in your eyes, and then you can come back, if we haven't already netted her. You might get some butter and salt on them chigger bites, too."

Malone asked for a status report from Unit 8. Unit 8 reported that the dogs had lost her most recent trail after three hundred yards and gave their new location. Malone asked for details and the rasping voice elaborated.

They had walked a long distance in a stream and neither the blood hounds or the handlers could pick up her exit point, though they had split up and ranged far in both directions. Malone thanked them and signed off.

The two Dalton City deputies sat on the hood of their car, watching the rest of the shift arrive. One deputy said, "They'll never catch her. She's too quick. Downright cunning. Must know every cave and cranny out there. If she holes up during the day and keeps moving only at night, no one's going to get her."

"Oh," said the other, "it's not like she can buy an airplane ticket and scoot to Brazil. Somebody's bound to run into her."

"Hope it ain't me or mine."

Ross Walker surveyed the countryside. She could be anywhere. Still, he had expected she'd be further away by now. From the coordinates of several places where they'd found her tracks, you'd think that she was traveling in a zigzaggy spiral, as if she really had nowhere to go.

THE NOISE of the monstrous propeller woke her, along with the terrible wind that kept the insect plane in the air.

MaryAnn slid further down into the water in the vast runoff tunnel as the helicopter eased down and held level with the huge circular opening under the highway, from which water cascaded fifty feet down to the streambed. Only her naked face remained above the waterline—not enough of a silhouette for her pursuers to spot. The copter hovered, then abruptly ascended, spewing pebbles and dirt into the vast tube. It droned off into the distance.

MaryAnn sat up in the stream water. She cupped some in her hands and drank. It was cold like snow and stung her flesh and made her shiver. A truck passing overhead shook the air. More heavy vehicles lumbered by. Normal people were so strong that they could live in the daytime, she thought. They were out there, going from place to place.

She hadn't meant to hide in the tunnel. It was a really stupid place. But she had been exhausted and thirsty, and the sun had risen fast while she dozed. And now she was caught here until sundown. The sun had always made her hide. Rising, she moved carefully along the stream of water to the end of the tunnel and looked out into the burning light. It smarted in her eyes and on the flesh of her face. Stepping further back into the shadows of the tunnel, she squatted and tried to defecate in the shallower water so as not to leave a spoor. Nothing came. What little she had scavenged as she ran was mostly green or tough, and had lodged deep in her gut. Peeing helped. Finished, she splashed herself with the cold water. It sent pleasure through her in the oddest way.

She splashed herself again, and again, then pressed her hand against the cold flesh until her fingers were warm and her body longed for the touch of skin. What was happening, she wondered. She did not have her hood on and did not care at that moment if someone saw her. She wanted only to touch herself and rock, like a baby. She closed her thighs on her hand and the sensation took her. She traced her body with her free hand and felt herself everywhere—everywhere—then moaned as the sensation caught her and carried her along, making her limbs hot, her breath short. She gasped and lay back against the curve of the tunnel, her head lolling to one side.

The freezing water felt good on her feet where briars and sticks and rocks had grazed her. She looked out again at the sun drenched forest. The light still hurt, but her eyes seemed able to fix themselves and she could look longer at the trees and rock outcroppings. She needed the night to hide inside. She was tired and still sleepy, but she couldn't sleep here. They would catch her. Despite the light, she would have to move, go deeper into the forest, perhaps cover herself again with moss and ferns, and smelly wild cabbage to fool the dogs, and there sleep under the cool vegetation until nightfall. Or find another hollow black gum tree to hide in.

But first she had to eat. From the plastic sling bag she took out her hood and a mangled wedge of flat, soggy bread that she had scavenged from a can behind a solitary house well off a wide paved road. It was splashed with pulpy looking sauce and shaped like a pie. She eyed it curiously and bit into it. It was rubbery but tasted like the cheese Mama sometimes brought home.

"Mama," she said, and heard her voice echo back.

THE GENTLE, circular motion of the helicopter lulled Sheriff Malone. Tyler Yates was the pilot, a veteran of missions over lots of dangerous green places. "You really going to shoot her?" he said over the intercom.

Malone peered through his binoculars at the pattern of tree tops. "Depends."

"On what?" Yates said.

"On whether I can hit her from this flying livingroom."

Yates shook his head.

"Listen," said Malone. "We've got a legal right and a legal obligation to bring down a fleeing felon if he or she refuses to surrender."

"But this is a teenager."

"So was Billy the Kid."

A slight sheen of perspiration covered Malone's face. He was chilled by the wind rushing by, yet hot at the same time. He glanced back at Leron Bervis, the deputy hanging over the side in the back seat, staring intently at the roof of green below them. Leron aspired to become the first black sheriff of Duncan County and concentrated hard on his tasks and his record. He sat back to back with another deputy at the other side door of the chopper. Against their hips rested the butts of high-powered rifles with telescopic sights. They brandished the weapons like supernaturally empowered phallic symbols. Every now and then, Leron sighted through his scope, using it instead of binoculars. Tyler Yates, glancing back, saw him hoist the rifle to his shoulder and peer through the crosshairs.

"You're not really going to gun her down, are you?" the pilot said.

"Hope not," Leron answered.

Malone said, "A lady school teacher almost bagged her last night with a .22 pistol. Caught the kid rummaging through her garbage. Thought it was raccoons going after stale pizza. The girl menaced her and growled and lit out, but not before the teacher got a couple of shots off."

"God," said Yates, "whatchya gotta go through for decent take-out these days."

"You wouldn't be jokin'," Malone said, "if you had seen the Lindsey boy."

"Sheriff!" Leron called out. "Down there."

"Where is there?" Yates said.

"There—where I'm pointin'"

"Three o'clock," Malone said. "She's running through a grove of pine at three o'clock."

The helicopter banked sharply to the right and the door on Leron's side was suddenly emptied of the horizon and filled with a picture of the ground. Yates rotated the helicopter around the spot Leron had seen the girl.

Malone snapped on the loudspeakers. *This is the Duncan County Sheriff's Department. You are ordered to surrender yourself into our custody. We will not harm you. We will not harm you.*

The figure shot across a small clearing and bounded into the trees.

"I lost her," Malone said.

"There," Leron exclaimed. "There she goes."

Leron leaned far out the open side and trained his sights on the running figure.

"She's really moving," Yates said into their headsets, not even bothering to disguise his delight.

"Damn, look at her go," Leron said. "I didn't think white people could run that fast."

A shot popped; they all strained to see. A clump of red earth, the size of a bowling ball, exploded right in front of her. She instantly changed direction.

"What is he doing?" Yates shouted.

"His job!" Malone yelled back.

Another shot popped, the noise mostly drowned out by the engine and rushing air.

"Bird One," Malone said into his mouthpiece, "this is Bird Two. Are you people sitting on your thumbs or what? We could use some help from your dogs over here. Suspect has been sighted near the stream diversion tunnel on Bessmer Road. She's partially in the open, heading for the woods. We're putting down."

The second helicopter acknowledged the call and Malone returned his attention to the small figure on the ground. She was covering a lot of territory fast. "Damn."

"What?" Yates said.

"Nothing."

The helicopter turned on an imaginary axis that was the girl's position. It rapidly descended, and the lone running figure grew larger and seemingly faster. Malone and everybody else aboard realized they would have no chance to catch her on the ground. It would be like chasing a wild animal. Only the dogs could keep up with her.

SHE IGNORED the brambles and tree limbs as she raced for the darkest part of the woods. She didn't feel her bleeding feet or the air blistering her lungs. The machine had landed and another was hovering. She ran and ran, leaping over felled trees, tearing through dead branches and scrub.

She came upon a stream a hundred times bigger than any she had ever seen and stopped. Her stomach convulsed at the abrupt halt but her lungs lapped air gratefully. She couldn't take another step and fell onto the hard bank, shaking violently as she fought to draw breath and made an involuntary sound as she gulped each one.

The hood was oppressive and she struggled to undo the front buttons, then folded it back so her mouth could more easily suck at the air. Men were shouting somewhere. Her chest heaved and heaved. The plastic sack was gone, along with the knife and the sweater. Her dress was rent in more places; half the bodice was held in place with a knot. She was sweating profusely and covered with chaff from the underbrush she had dashed through.

Her pulse slowed; the pain in her side subsided. She scuttled over to the stream's edge and drank a handful of water, then waded in, heading for the far side. By the third stride, she couldn't feel the bottom. The fast water caught her and pulled her down. Water was everywhere, pushing her downstream. In all her life she had never been in water deeper than her knees.

THEY FOUND MaryAnn's trail again more than three hundred yards south of where the dogs had lost it. A quarter of mile further south, after a dog-leg turn east, they lost it again. Leron complained that the girl was truly unnatural. They'd had her spotted and were on the ground in less than a minute, and yet she'd vanished so completely, the hounds couldn't even agree on a direction.

Ross Walker was bushed. There was no telling how old the trail was. The only thing he knew clearly now was that she did not have a destination or a plan, other than simple evasion. She had led them all over Creation, heading steadily away from her home, only to double back on them and circle around. It was impossible to intercept her because it was impossible to guess where she was going from one minute to the next. Hell, he thought, why not stop chasing all over the woods and just sit and wait for her to show. Not a strategy likely to be adopted, however.

It was six forty-five, with the sun pouring over the western horizon. They were stalled. Stumped, at least temporarily. Malone had already cycled out nearly half of the searchers, leaving a token crew scattered around the countryside, ostensibly to protect the citizens of Duncan County after hours. Now Malone ordered the rest of them to their beds, and this included Ross, who wanted to continue a while longer.

"No sense," Malone said. "You haven't so much as taken a piss break since coming on. You look terrible. Go home. I'll see y'all at sunrise."

On its second trip, Bird One took him out. It was eight minutes to the staging area, where he'd left his car.

Knowing he would take a long time to wind down, Ross drove back to the Nelson place to see what the search coordinator there might have divined or heard on his electronic grapevines. But when he reached the turnoff at the mailbox, he saw the gates were chained shut and the familiar "crime scene" ribbons posted in front of them. Ross pulled his car to the side of the road, just behind Jimmy Lowell's cruiser and next to Matt's. Matt was back monitoring the radios and marking the map he now had spread open across most of the front seat. Other maps of other quadrants lay open across the backrest.

Matt was waiting for his relief. They'd given up on using the Nelson place: too hard to get to. Jimmy Lowell was going on duty with the next shift. He had driven Lola out to meet up with Ross and she had talked Lowell into escorting her up to the Nelson house. Ross said he might just take a hike up there, too, and ducked under the day-glo ribbon in front of the gate and squeezed through the gap left by the slack in the chain that held the gate closed.

The trek up to the house was much longer than he remembered, or maybe he was just that tired. The woods were also more ominous on foot at dusk than they were in a vehicle. He undid the loop on his sidearm and slid the flashlight off his belt, in case. He was slightly embarrassed by his precautions. But he took them anyway.

When he reached the last rise before the house, he saw Jimmy Lowell sitting on a chopping log, alone. The two hailed each other and Jimmy came forward to greet him.

"Have a nice stroll?" he said.

"My evening constitutional," Ross replied. "What with my sedentary job, I like a brisk walk to set me up for a good night's rest."

Jimmy laughed and the two of them walked back toward the house, Jimmy explaining that he had brought Lola out in the hope of locating her boyfriend. Lowell himself was due on night time duty out by I-75. The radius of the search, he explained, had widened to nearly thirty miles. Despite the optimistic predictions of Sheriff Malone's spokesperson, nobody really knew where MaryAnn was, where she had been, or when she had been there.

"If the girl don't starve to death first," Lowell said, "'Mad Mike' Malone might keep us out here until next winter."

"Where's Lola?" Ross said.

Jimmy Lowell pointed to the well worn path leading up to the barn.

"Duty calls," he said and after high-fiving with his former high school classmate, he strode away down the bumpy track toward the highway.

Ross walked up to the barn and hailed her from outside. She stepped out, smiling, and they embraced.

"Don't you smell randy," she teased.

"You have something against skunk cabbage?"

She laughed and held her nose, while he squeezed her close and nipped her neck.

"So what are you doing out here?" he said.

"Looking for my lost love, and snooping."

He nodded. "What did you find in the barn?"

"More bones, glass bottles, sculptures, odd thatch dolls

with feathers and things protruding from them. Did Jimmy tell you what the helicopter cops found?"

"No."

"Jimmy saw pictures of it. A round field. It's not too far from where the abandoned car was found. The field has all sorts of odd stuff around it and three circular pits—two the same, one a bit smaller." She squatted down drew it in the dirt with her finger, then stood again. "Look familiar?"

"Yeah," Ross said. "The faces on the wall of her room, and the thing at Endicott's that she had made."

"Right."

He looked back down at the picture she had drawn. "A giant face."

"Yes, with no features, and facing up."

"Mad people's art is pretty compelling," Ross said. "Creepy, too."

Hands on her hips, Lola looked out over the darkening homestead. "Sure is."

"Well," he said. "No luck at all today. It's getting harder by the hour. Her endurance is amazing. She's like an animal with a human's cunning. Mike Malone's scared stiff she'll pop up in someone's kitchen to raid the ice box or the garbage and kill some more taxpayers. Today he had the helicopter guys pack sniper rifles. They got off a couple of shots, too."

"Oh, no," Lola said, her voice pained. "This is someone who needs every kind of help. Instead we've unleashed an armed posse."

Ross sighed. "Not much we can do about it at the moment. Let's head out of here before the light's completely gone."

"I kind of had other plans," she said.

"Like what?"

She reached back inside the barn and drew out a sleeping roll.

"Are you crazy or what?" he said.

"No. I thought about this a lot. I thought about her a lot—all day. There's only one place she has in the whole world, and only one person."

"Her mom."

"Yeah."

"And you think she'll come looking for her?"

"Yeah."

"And you propose to camp out here until this deranged person makes for home?"

"Yeah."

"And you think I'm gonna rough it out here with you."

"Yeah."

"Hell," Ross said. "Back in high school I chickened out of staying the night in a haunted house in town, and you think I'm going to last the night on the ground in this asylum?"

Lola shrugged. "Somebody's got to. You know her mama won't."

Ross puffed up his cheeks, and breathed deeply. "Yeah."

"I'll make it worth your while," she said and rose up on her toes to kiss him.

SHE WATCHED them mate. They were noisy, like cats. Their bodies arched the same way, too. But they smelled different. The woman's perfume grew stronger as they did it. Afterward their scent was entirely different—chalky sort of, ordinary.

They did it soon again, emitting smaller noises this time. MaryAnn felt her pulse race. Her mouth was open, tongue out to better catch the scents. She did something to him—it was hard to see what—and he cried out. When the two were finished, they slept.

What were they doing in the barn? Where was Mama?

MaryAnn waited for the moon to come up.

11

LOLA AND Ross were curled together like spoons. Ross slept without moving, completely exhausted. Lola had trouble falling asleep. His arm beneath her head was somehow uncomfortable. She propped herself on one elbow to deal with it and discovered the reason for her discomfort was his pistol. He had fallen asleep with it in his left hand, by her head; his right lay inert across her chest. She picked the weapon up daintily, with two fingers and placed it just outside the sleeping bag, then curled back inside and pulled his arm back across her breasts and shut the folds of the bag.

Sleep enveloped her in moments. She dreamed of her uncle in New York and Quetzalcoatl. Both were oddly coiffed with wonderous feathers and pranced like show girls. Uncle Gus drew nearer and spoke to her in hushed tones, suggesting she might want to wake up. Which she did—with a start, her eyes popping open.

Nothing but darkness and a little bit of moonlight. The barn was empty. Why, she wondered, hadn't Muriel Nelson kept any livestock? Not so much as a chicken. How had she gotten by financially? Endicott had said she refused all suggestions of aid from him or welfare assistance, taking seeming pleasure in his knowing how bare of even small luxuries their lives were here. Yet clearly she had some cash. It was all very well to forage clothes and saleable scraps from the dump and from roadsides, but the taxes alone on property this size ran into the thousands each year. It didn't add up to a fortune, but for someone who had no visible income at all and no bank account for the past twelve years, it must have been an insurmountable sum. How had she financed their existence out here?

Lola closed her eyes and inhaled deeply. All was quiet as she peacefully lay in the arms of the man she had not expected to find in her life. They had come into each other's lives so easily, she thought. It was pretty evident he loved her and, despite her own misgivings after her recent divorce, she had to admit she loved the guy.

Her eyes opened involuntarily. A reflex. Something was in the barn. A mouse? Shit—a rat, she thought, and hoped it was a raccoon. She would visualize a raccoon. Georgia was loaded with raccoons, even the towns. At camp once, in the Pocono Mountains, she and her bunkmates had been visited by a skunk. She would pretend this was a raccoon and not think about it further. Live and let live.

She wished Ross had gone along with sleeping in the Nelson house but he'd adamantly refused. He said it wouldn't do if her theory proved right and the girl turned up, but she suspected it was simply because the house creeped him out. Not that the converted barn was uncomfortable. It had obviously been Muriel's studio once. Yellowing canvasses were stored high overhead in the exposed rafters, although they hadn't been protected from the leaky roof or the barn mice. She'd been curious to view them, but neither she nor Ross had had the energy to wrestle them down the rickety ladder. Morning would do.

The moonlight grew more distinct. Blurs in the darkness took on edges and even grew shadows. That noise again—gnawing. Was it growing louder, or maybe it just wasn't far away. She squinted to focus better, then tried the opposite, widening her eyes to let in more light. Not much scientific basis, she thought, but what the hell.

The sound died away. Goodnight raccoon. But the diner took shape. A large blurry mass as black as the wall against which it was propped. How far? Twenty-five, thirty feet?

She mildly pinched the flesh on the arm laid across her chest. No response. She pinched harder. He grunted and his breathing changed. She dug a nail in and he tensed. He was awake and instantly cognizant somehow of her fear. His arm, slung across her chest, moved gently as his hand felt around for the pistol.

She didn't dare speak. Instead, she took his hand by the wrist and guided it out of the sleeping bag toward where the gun was, beside their heads. He got the message and swept the floor with his hand.

The hunched creature drew nearer, five paces away. It made no sound at all, except the munching. She could make out the squatting silhouette, her hair a lusturous white, ravenously eating something from the lap of her dress, Ross's pistol hanging upside down from a finger.

"MaryAnn," Lola said.

The eating stopped.

"We've been waiting for you."

The meal was discarded. The girl moved laterally—still squatting—and stopped. The sleeping bag lay almost directly in the middle of the floor. She was no closer, but had moved nearer their heads.

Lola pushed herself up a little, her arm came out of the bag. "We were worried about you."

There was no response.

In a happy voice, Lola said, "I'll tell you what, honey. Can you help me get this lantern lit?" She had said it but made no motion to do it. Neither did MaryAnn. Then MaryAnn spoke.

"What did you do with Mama?"

"Your mother?"

"I want her."

"Of course."

"Everybody's chasing me."

"Yes."

"Everybody hates me."

"They don't. Not really."

"What's your name?"

"Ahh . . . Lola. Lola Aragon."

"Portugese?"

"Spanish."

"Do you sail?"

"No. I've never sailed."

"The Spanish were great sailors, too."

"Yes." There was a tremor in Lola's voice.

"Have you got another gun?"

"No," Lola said. "That's the only one."

"Those boys shot at me. They killed Benjees."

"I know. That's why we came to find you, to make sure you were safe."

"Is he a policeman? Why did he have a gun?"

"Yes," Ross said. "I am."

MaryAnn shifted laterally again to have a better view of him.

"I'm going to sit up," Ross said and paused. When there was no objection, he slid halfway out of the bag and sat upright. Lola eased herself up, too.

"My Mama," MaryAnn said. "Tell me where she is?"

"She's with God," Ross said.

The white-haired head swiveled in the dark for a moment, then spoke. "Mama said there was no God."

"Do you think that, too?" Lola said.

"I'm not a baby," MaryAnn said.

"You're an intelligent young woman," Lola said. "And an artist."

"Mama is an artist." MaryAnn said. "I just build things." She raised the pistol. "Will this gun kill?"

"It can," Ross said, "yes. But it's not supposed to."

"Did a policeman kill Mama?"

"Yes," Ross said, hoarsely.

"You?"

"No, not me. Another policeman. A new one who didn't know he was doing a wrong thing."

"If you had the gun and I ran away now, you could shoot me, yes?"

"I wouldn't."

She smacked the gun barrel against the floor. "You would! You would! Say you would."

"Policemen carry guns to protect themselves and other people. Policemen aren't hunters, they—."

"They hunt *me*," she said.

"MaryAnn," Lola said, "we want to help you—very much. We would like you to come with us. We don't want anyone to harm you."

"I don't want to live in a zoo."

"We won't take you to a zoo."

"I don't want to be in a circus."

"No. No circus."

Ross said, "Did you come back here to stay, MaryAnn?"

She grunted. "No. I can't be here anymore. The boys are gone. Mama is gone. And they're still looking for me in the woods." She held the metal of the gun against her cheek for a moment. "I came for money. I need to go to the Arctic."

"The Arctic," Ross whispered.

"Yes. It's dark there—all the time."

"Where is the money?"

MaryAnn looked at him, then at her. "You get the money."

"How?" Lola said. "I don't have too much with me."

"I'll show you." She motioned for Lola to come. "You," she said to Ross. "Stay."

"I will. I promise."

She pushed the battery lantern toward Lola. "Take it."

Lola complied

"Stand."

Lola stood.

"Don't turn it on until I say."

"All right."

"You shouldn't need it. Over there—" She pointed to the large stone fireplace behind them. Lola went to it and stood by the mantel. It was a huge old hearth. MaryAnn moved a few feet closer like a crab, and closer still, until she was squatting beside Lola. The girl reeked.

"Go inside," MaryAnn said to Lola.

"What?"

"Go in."

Ross said, "She means step inside the fireplace."

"All right," Lola said and—hunched over—felt her way to the fieldstone face and groped until she had found the large opening, then shuffled inside. She remained stooped, her body white against the darkness of it.

"Stand up," MaryAnn said.

"What! I can't."

"Lola." Ross enunciated very slowly. "There's a long, narrow space above you. It's smaller than the area you're in, because the mouth tapers, just above your head. The smoke rises up through a narrower opening, like a throat. There's a ledge there. If you stand up into that opening in the throat, you'll see it, or feel it." He looked at Maryann. "Is that right, MaryAnn."

"Yes. The money's there, on the ledge. There are boxes of it. They'll be on your left, facing in. I just want one. Don't use the lamp unless I say. Left!"

"Okay, okay," Lola said, "left," her voice oddly muffled yet echoing. Her head disappeared from her body. "It's tight in here."

"You alright?" Ross said.

"Yeah, I just can't move my head all that much."

"Feel around.

Debris pelted the fireplace. Lola coughed. "The creosote is getting me."

"Find it?" Ross said.

"No." Lola choked. "I can't—"

MaryAnn rocked—agitated. "It's on the left."

"Can I turn on the light?" Lola said.

MaryAnn didn't answer.

"Can she turn on the light?" Ross asked, loud enough for Lola to hear, too.

"Yes," Mary Ann said, "but only shine it up in the hole."

A shaft of light shot down from inside the chimney and Lola screamed and kept screaming. Creosote and debris rained down, loose chinking fell, then things cascaded down around her, until she all but disappeared in the dust. Ross leaped into the opening and barely got her out before the interior ledge gave way. They came stumbling over the piles of bones and wallets and good sized stones dribbling out of the throat of the chimney. A large stone crashed down. A skull bounced with a terrible, hollow sound, then another. Fillings gleamed in their rictal grins. A pelvis clattered into the fireplace. A boney arm swung down and back and forth like a pendulum. The lantern finally fell, too, and the light went out.

Lola shook in Ross's embrace. Objects stopped falling, except for a stream of sandy debris they could hear.

"Sorry," MaryAnn said in the dark. "It was a bad idea anyway. The Arctic is only dark half the time. I'm not sure the forests go that far north anyhow. I wouldn't have any way to get there." She fell silent for some moments. "You don't like bones," she said.

Lola's voice trembled: "Not particularly."

"Mama never let me have these," MaryAnn said. "Is there blood? Is your skin bruised? Your body is so soft," she said, sounding annoyed.

"I . . . I'm sorry you don't like it," Lola half-whispered, trying to control the tremor in her chest.

"It's all right," MaryAnn said. "He likes it."

"Would you like to go somewhere you can build things?" Ross said.

"No!"

"Is there something we can do to help you?" he said.

"Yes." MaryAnn became animated. "Yes!" She crept closer.

Lola's heart pounded. The muzzle of the pistol gaped at them. Ross' skin was hot against hers. She felt him tense. Don't lunge, she thought. Don't scare her. There was no way he was going to take away the gun. Not before she fired.

Ross said, very evenly, "How can we help you, MaryAnn?"

She held the pistol extended in both hands, elbows resting on her knees. The metal ground like gears as she cocked the hammer.

"MaryAnn—" Lola sounded breathless. "We want to to help, if you'll just say how."

"Kill me," she said happily. "Kill me."

"MaryAnn!" Lola said with disbelief. "MaryAnn."

Ross reached out slowly and took hold of the barrel, then waited for MaryAnn to release her grip. When she did, he exhaled and turned the gun away.

"I want to go to Mama," she said.

Lola inched closer and touched the girl's knee. "I need to hold you for a moment," she said. "May I."

MaryAnn brushed Lola's fingers with the back of hers in a curious, distant way. She felt Lola's knuckles.

"Will they beat me?"

"No one's going to beat you," Lola said.

"Never," Ross added. "Not anyone." He was slipping into his pants.

Lola eased the girl into her arms. MaryAnn curled up like a small creature and let herself be rocked. "I'm very tired," she said, and Lola could feel the truth of it in the body she held. The girl was completely spent. The lips against her thigh were swollen and cracked. She could feel her slip away into merciful sleep, a misshapen child dreaming of escaping her misshapen life.

Ross snapped on the fluorescent tube of a battery lantern and the room turned flat in the white light.

"Holy hell," he said, bringing the light closer.

Lola looked up at him, the girl a fetal ball in her lap. He was staring wide-eyed at MaryAnn, mouth agape. He knelt on one knee in front of them, looking aghast.

"What, Ross?"

"She's beautiful," he said.

12

THE BORDER terrier gamboled across Dr. Endicott's lawn, pursued by Dr. Endicott's daughter. Her platinum hair flew as she chased the little dog, imitating perfectly its snarls and barks, even flipping back her lips to match its fierce aspect. Lola watched her for a moment, then turned her attention back to their host. He, too, was following the girl's pursuit of his pet.

"Loco hasn't been the same since she got here," he said and laughed. "She really keeps him running. I've never seen anyone so fast."

Ross nodded agreement. "She could have had an interesting athletic career."

"How could I have been such a fool?" Endicott said wistfully. "And how could Muriel have been so vengeful?"

"Muriel fooled everyone," Lola said. "She worked for a lot of years at that studio in California, right next door to the special makeup artists. And you know how good an artist she was herself."

"Also ruthless," Ross said. "She financed her vengeance in pretty hideous fashion. All that rage drowned her, and a lot of innocent people."

Endicott looked sad for a moment. "How could she have done that to her own child, and taken lives simply for money? She could have had all she wanted from me."

"I don't think that's what she wanted from you," Lola said. "What she craved was recognition. She blamed you for her failing to achieve it and committed herself totally to your anguish. The anger fueled her, and fed on her. You couldn't have swayed Muriel. She wanted you to suffer, even if her daughter had to as well."

"I was a coward," Endicott said. "Let's not put too fine a point on it. MaryAnn could have grown up normally if I hadn't been scared off by her mother. My weakness of character was there to be played on. But I shall make my penance and hope it's enough to undo some of the harm that befell MaryAnn. I can't tell you how grateful I was for your testimony at the preliminary hearing."

Lola smiled. "She's changed so much in these months."

At the end of the garden, MaryAnn was on all fours in front of the growling terrier, a napkin on her head, hiding her face. She stayed perfectly still as the dog crept closer, unable to resist its own curiosity.

"Boo!" she said, and the dog erupted with barks, as she collapsed in gales of laughter.